Sixes Wild:
Echoes

I0680581

By Tempe O'Kun

FURPLANET®

Dallas, TX

Sixes Wild: Echoes

Production © FurPlanet Productions

Copyright © 2016 by Tempe O'Kun

Cover © Shinigamigirl
Character icons © Yuki-chi
"Rough Ride" © Slate
"Storm Clouds" © Hibbary
"Showing a Pair" © Yuki-chi
"Wing and a Hare" © Yuki-chi
"Turnabout" © Shinigamigirl
"Laying in Wait" © Slate
"Coyote Orb" © DarkNatasha
"Tea Cup" © Chromamancer

Chapter 11 of this book won the 2014 Bronze Typewriter Award for Best Western Story when released as a preview.

Editors: Carl Minez, Eliot Wro, Kohaku Nightfang, Sillyneko, Slate, Slip-Wolf, Sophie.

Published by FurPlanet Productions
Dallas, TX
http://www.FurPlanet.com

ISBN 978-1-61450-325-5

Printed in the United States of America
First Edition Trade Paperback 2016

To Sophie, for the courage.
To Megan, for the sass.

Contents

Chapter 1

Her face emerges from the front opening, giving her the appearance of an irate, bunny-eared turtle.

My thief, a hare with a gunbelt and a grin, saunters into the office. Her pelt's as brown as dusty leather and white as clean cotton. She's a tall thing, wiry as a telegraph line and twice as electrifying. A booted kick clatters the door shut after her. Her smirk shines down at me, like one second of being here strikes out a month of being gone.

A rush like vertigo swoops through me. I straighten as much as my chair allows. My feet are up on the desk, wings crossed as I reclined. I'd been in the middle of correspondence. "Six."

"Lawbat." She tips her hat brim up with a clawed thumb. A gleam of silver and metallic blue catch the sunlight at either hip.

A long moment passes through the White Rock sheriff's office. Outside, the citizenry clatters and chatters by, unaware their local constabulary is feeling outclassed by a doe bunny in trousers. My heart demands I leap up to kiss her, but I'm caught at a crosswind of emotion. A whole month she's been wild and in the wind. Were I not a gentleman, I'd have strong words for her. Were I not obligated to keep the town safe, I'd have been on the wing after her. "Thought you had a lion to run down."

"Hayes has gone to ground. Haven't got mah gun back either." Panting, she winks. "'Bout the only thing that could turn my month around is you."

With a wry look, I grab a canteen from beside my desk. It sloshes, half full, as I toss it to her.

She catches it, spins the cap off, and gulps greedily. We have this easy read on each other. It calls to mind scandalous moments of cooperation.

For the hundredth time, I want to ask her to stay, but can't think of any means to justify such an imposition. I retreat to niceties. "Lovely to see you. Pleasant day, isn't it?"

A few swallows later, she swings the canteen from her lips. The wind whistling past its opening tells me it's emptied. "Ah!" She wipes her muzzle. "Much obliged, Blake." She hangs the vessel by its strap on my hat rack. The steel cap, strung on a length of cord, drums to mark time as the canteen swings. "Drier 'an a saloon on nickel night out there."

Twirling the pen with my feet, I steeple my wing fingers. "To what do I owe the pleasure?"

Her boots tap along the floorboards, then grind an inch of grit as she spins on a heel to face me. Her grin gleams. "Ah need a reason to visit?"

I roll my eyes. "So it would seem."

A flicker of sadness steals that smile, which I feel a pang of guilt about. But then she bounces back, leaning beside the window, blue eyes like a glimpse at the sky. One fuzzy digit rises. "Ah have a notion."

"Dare I ask?" Twirling the pen between my toes, I try to focus on my paperwork. Got a telegram about some martens calling themselves the Pine City Gang, who could well be in my area. White Rock needs a good sheriff. I like to think I fit the bill, yet I get precious little done when she's around. She always has illicit little plans for me.

She rests her paws on those revolvers, one a silver heirloom, the other a blue steel substitute. "A spot of treasure hunting."

I look up from my bookkeeping to take account of Six. One never can tell how serious she takes her tomfoolery.

"Ah've been hearin' rumors." She brushes the dust from her fluffy tail. "Folk tell of a cliff-house with all manner of lost riches."

With a sigh, I lean back in my chair, steeple my wings, and put away the pen with one foot. "I wouldn't put much stock in saloon scuttlebutt."

"Nor would ah, but ah heard it from an old 'yote traveling with the circus."

My wing fingers interlace. I wish I knew her better, and not just because I'd like to know if she's poking fun at me. "If he knew where all this treasure was, why was he traveling with a circus?"

"He said it was cursed." Her dextrous paws dance theatrically. "Everybody who went lookin' met a grisly end."

"So, naturally, you want to go there posthaste and ensnare yourself in said curse."

"Utter hokum-bunkum." Her smile implies I'm the harebrained one here. "No such thing as curses."

I tap a wing finger to my lips, contemplating, then point it her way. "You're carrying around a gun that gives you visions of your father's ghost."

"Bein' helpfully haunted leaves me suited to suss out the truth in such matters." She pats the silver gun. "The true shine on the matter's this: the supposed cache is hardly a day's travel from here."

"Big desert out there, Six."

"Which is why ah helped mahself to a look around." The hare cocks her hips with a creak of gunbelt leather. "After a few days, these little titters a' mischief kept pricklin' mah ears, right at the edge of hearin'."

"And you'd finally lost your faculties."

"Mah faculties are found and firmly fixed, thank you." Her arms cross, little curls of dust trailing off in the sunbeam she splits. "Took me a spell to figure out it wasn't a sound: just a notion buzzin' in the stone. 'Yotes love buildin' near mirror ore, and that means…"

Still spinning the pen with my toes, I point it her way. "…echoes."

"Just that. So ah picked mahself up from the dirt where ah'd collapsed and high-tailed it back here." She jerked her thumb at the window, toward the sweaty pony tied to the post outside. I recognize it as Pumpernickel, the bay she stole from me a while ago. "Figure that means mah lead's golden. Who knows what else might be?"

"And I'm along to, what? Drag you back when the echoes overwhelm your well-tenured faculties?"

"To ensure mah sweet little bunny self doesn't come to harm." She shines me a look of great innocence. "And help me carry the loot back."

A laugh flies from my muzzle. "I strive not to burglarize my neighborhood." I straighten my vest, finding a tiny spot of jam from breakfast, and scraping it away with a claw. "You ought to try it sometime."

"But there's the crux, Blake: the 'yotes don't live there." Her fingertip traces along the brim of that hat, drawing my gaze to the stormy blues under its shade. "Never have. Some other band left it long ago."

My ears droop at her tall tale. "Why would they leave their treasures behind?"

"Can't say ah'm well versed in the ways of natives. You'd have to ask yer deputy." She waves a paw in the vague direction of the town. "Probably outta respect for their ancestors or some such."

I press a thumb and finger to my eyes, then slide them down my muzzle. "And it's just waiting for an enterprising hare to happen upon it?"

"If she has a bat's-eye view on matters." Boots squeaking the floorboards, she ambles toward me.

"I'm very much in doubt of any treasure, bewitched or otherwise, hidden in the mountains." I gesture to the hills beyond my tidy office. "They've been heavily prospected, back during the silver rush."

She plants her paws on my desk and leans in with a poker-face smile. "If yer so dead-set there's no trouble to be had, then ya ought to have no objection to comin' with me."

I chuckle. My old law professors would never forgive me if I bungled into so obvious a rhetorical trap. "I hardly think that follows."

Those stormy eyes meet mine. Her ears droop over the brim of her hat. Something sweet grows in the gravel of her voice. "Ah'll owe ya a day."

My heart skips a beat, then capers through several more.

"'Sides…" She winks. "It'll give ya some notion of how exciting and dangerous mah life is."

I roll my eyes, resigned to following her on this little adventure. If nothing else, it should be a chance to spend time with the slippery thief.

⅄ ≈ ⅄

Desert winds sweep under my wings as I swoop down to a landing. Red dust scatters in a double arc. The rocky ground burns under my feet.

Six stands up from a bolder she'd been seated on, flicking her cigarette into the scree. "Well?"

I straighten my vest. This new one always rides up when I fly. Then I smile at her. "Your quest may not be a fool's errand after all."

Those shapely ears popping upward, she perks up bodily. "You saw something?"

"I saw a tumbledown entrance to a cliff dwelling. No stairs to speak of and it's tucked away in a gully." My wings fold up with a flourish. "I can see why a non-flighted treasure hunter would miss it."

"Gettin' fonder a' those wings all the time." Silken paws run up their membranes, against the grain of the fine hairs there.

I shiver, then stretch my wings for another flight. "Give me a launch, would you?"

"Surely will, lawbat." She crouches to let me hop on her shoulders. Once she has me at a disadvantage, her ears spring up against the front of my trousers. "You know ah'll get ya up anytime."

Warmth rushes my cheeks and ears, having nothing to do with the pleasant heat of the day. The next instant, she bounces, hard, and propels me skyward. In my discombobulated state, I require a few awkward flaps to get the currents under me. Having taken to the air, I spiral up on the desert drafts to the top of a mesa. I land and regain my composure. That hare beams her wiles at me with the regularity of a lighthouse, and yet I'm still shocked by their power when they catch me by surprise.

Half an hour's tough climb and rougher language later, Six manages to follow. She claws her way to the crest and takes a swig from her canteen. From there, I lead her on a jaunt across the tops of the buttes.

She seems not overly conversational, and I can't think of anything to say. I let the conversation slacken. We hike on in silence, though I do stay grounded to encourage her. My ears perk as her boot steps slow. "Six?" I turn.

Staggering, she swoons into a lopsided dance. Her voice trails off in a mumble. Dust scuffs up from her shuffled steps as she teeters on the brink of a fall.

For an instant, I think the desert hare's finally succumbed to heat sickness, but then pluck a few words from her muttering.

"Ah can't understand y'all when ya yap at once." She swipes a paw at empty space, then keels casually over. "Confounded yotes…"

I scramble to prop her up. "Whoa now!" With her half-draped over me, I slow our crash landing. Now seated on the dirt, sparkles of silver on the ground catch my eye. I'd bet my best jar of black currant jelly that it's mirror ore. I turn my attention to the senseless bunny. Not eager to carry her the rest of the way, I rattle her by the shoulders. "Hey!"

Her blue eyes blink open. She shakes her head, ears flopping. "Gettin' noisy up here..."

I notice the half-buried remains of a structure here, adobe and stone built up in piles that'd looked natural from a distance. Must have been a 'yote dwelling of some kind. I throw her arm over my shoulder and press on. With considerable effort, I manage to drag her to her feet and further along the butte. A few dozen yards away, the ground stops twinkling.

As we put distance between ourselves and the ore dust, Six's ears slowly rise. Her weight leaves my shoulders. "Beg yer pardon, lawbat." She straightens with an abashed expression, adjusts her collar, and fluffs her tail. "Just some ghosts gettin' the drop on me."

"I don't suppose they mentioned anything of use?"

"'Fraid not." She props her paw on the silver pistol at her hip. A blue steel replacement glints at the other, though not as bright. "Echoes aren't as direct as a telegram."

"Pity." I give her another glance, watching for any residual signs of ore exposure. "Come on. It's not much further."

Another hundred yards, then we trudge up shallow a scree slope. I flutter here and there, the occasional pointy rock punishing my lack of boots. At last, we reach a gray crumble of canyon. Bands of red rock stand exposed here, like much of the rest of the territory, but close inspection reveals the obvious sheer marks of tools.

"Why're we stoppin'?" She pants. Her paws prop against her knees as she looks up at me between wilted ears.

I sweep a wing at our destination. "Your treasure cave, madam."

"That's a pile a' rocks, lawbat." A sour look crosses her sweet muzzle. "Ah could've found the same on the desert floor."

After some scrambling and squabbling, I take her by the shoulders and glide to the entrance. She hollers the whole way, even after I deposit her in a dusty and irregular doorway.

Exquisite murals run the walls, carvings of desert tortoises in fantastical scenarios. Some are emerging from the Earth, others are taking the shape of mountains. "This is truly fascinating. This tribe must have revered them for their ability to survive in the desert."

"Never found them overburdened with wit." Her glance casts over the carvings. She adjusts the coil of rope slung over her shoulder. "Ah had one scuttle up to squat in my shadow. Thought ah was a shade tree."

"I can attest you're a shady character. Though it is quite pleasant under your shade." I fondle her supple ears, like the leaves of some exotic plant.

"You keep yer wings to yourself, mister." She swats my wing away. "Ah know when ah'm bein' sassed."

We walk deeper into the dark passage. With a climate this dry, it's tough to determine just how long the place has been abandoned. One would expect the air to have the musty mold of ancient decay, but it's scarcely dustier than outside and cooler to a refreshing degree.

Six pulls a torch and matchbox from her bag of treasure-seeking supplies. Balancing, I hold the torch helpfully in one foot as she strikes a match and sheds light on our exploits. Topaz, lapis, and aquamarine glint from the mosaics of the walls. Six takes the torch back with barely a glance at the astounding artwork, and we press on.

My first inkling that something's amiss comes when those murals begin to change. Gone are the depictions of placid desert-dwelling tortoises; ominous looking snappers take their place, jagged maws gaping menacingly.

"Let's get to that treasure." She fairly bounces down the tunnel. Her boots make a steady stamp down the echoing space.

I spy a glimmer of metal in one of the lower alcoves. In the dim light, I see the faint outline of a tortoise statuette, about knee-high. With such dry air, it too appears untouched by time.

Her boot clomps down on a rounded bulge on the floor. The tile emits a soft click. The grind of stone reverberates from the wall.

My wing seizes her shoulder, yanking her back.

A flash of copper lurches in front of us.

Snap!

The mechanical turtle chomps shut with enough force to curl dust from its body.

Six jumps about three feet in the air, head almost hitting the ceiling. "What in blue blazes!"

"Put those pretty ears of your to use." I point at the tile she compressed.

As the mechanical guardian retreats on its little track, the stone rises with another soft click. The passage stands as harmless as ever.

She hikes one foot at a time to check that they're undamaged. "Who puts a leg-chompin' beast like that in a burrow?"

After checking for any additional plates, I kneel to examine the mechanism. The trap sits in its alcove, quite inert. It's made of copper, with a ceramic overlay on the shell. "I suspect it's part of the tortoise motif. This is a temple, after all."

"Ah suspect ah don't give a thin dime about their motifs. Any turtles fixin' for a taste a' me are mah personal shooting gallery." She checks her guns. "Ah say we make a break for it, hop the whole way, and crack any teapots we find taking liberties."

"On the contrary, my dear Six Shooter." I raise a wing finger, invoking a tone often used by my old professors. "We're going to take to heart the lesson this temple is meant to teach us."

She lifts one ear at me. "Meanin' what, exactly?"

"Slow and steady wins the race." I lead her very slowly past the snapping turtle trap.

"That's just somethin' slow folk say." Even as she sasses me, her eyes never leave the floor, searching for more loose tiles. The dust makes it difficult, obscuring all but the widest gaps in the floor.

"I am simply offering you the best chance at getting through this tunnel unbitten."

The bunny's expression darkens as she alights on the realization I might be right. She grumbles after me in the dim passage, lit only by the occasional air shaft.

We continue on and on. After an hour of patient progress, we clear the last of the alcoves. Around us, the tunnel opens into a small, round chamber. I give a laugh of relief. "Not quite how I pictured this adventure."

The gunslinger regards me with sour peevishness. She passes by a strange, notched pole near the center of the room. She comes to the far end of the space, finds a round portal and gives the tortoise-tail handle a shake.

It doesn't budge.

I try to inspire her to patience by demonstration. An inspection of the gloom above me shows strange protrusions in a domed ceiling.

She tries the handle again, harder, but equally negative results. "It's jammed."

"Or locked." I scratch under my chin, studying the carvings ringing the room. "These engravings could hold the key."

"Aren't any hinges on this side, so it's gotta open the other way." She throws her weight against the door. Again, to no effect.

"Slow down." The etchings show all manner of celestial tortoises. By the light of the air vents, I can see they trace all around the walls. "You might be tough as old leather, but the traps in this place would stamp you with more than a decorative pattern."

"The floor in here doesn't have those loose tiles." She swings a solid kick against the barrier. Nothing. "Should be fine." Bracing against the notched pole, she hops up to deliver a massive wallop to the door with both feet.

From the ceiling with an echoing clatter, a massive copper turtle shell rattles down. It covers the cussing hare in an instant, clacking to the floor. Furious scrambling rattles around inside it.

A step back toward the tunnel saves me from similar entrapment. I walk toward her, tapping with care on the shell. "You okay in there?"

Her face emerges from the front opening, giving her the appearance of an irate, bunny-eared turtle. "Do ah look okay to you?"

I laugh. The situation is too absurd to do otherwise.

"Blast it all, Blake!" Struggle as she might, she can't force her shoulders through. "Ah've had mah fill a' this whole fluff-mattin' consarn!"

Stifling my amusement, I wipe a tear from my eye. "Just relax. This has to have some kind of catch."

"Ah'm not waitin' for you to poke around." She grunts with the effort of another full-strength bunny-kick. The shell barely shivers. "That tears it—ah'm shootin' mah way outta this overgrown teacup." A gun clicks inside the heavy stone enclosure.

"Don't do that." My wing fingers tap their way along the massive shell. The shell's engraved surface has been inlayed with turquoise to form a single continuous mosaic. "The bullet's just as likely to just bounce around and hit you."

Head still poking from the shell, she sinks into sullen grumbles.

With a cautious eye out for any secondary trap that could spring out at me, I lean over the shell. "It looks to have a catch, but it's not exposed here. See if you can reach it from the inside."

She fumbles around inside the shell, then a loud click rattled through the chamber. Her next kick against the heavy copper shell shifted it. After great effort, we managed to lift one side high enough for her to slip free through the hole. She stood, flustered and fur mussed.

I patted her shoulder, dust puffing off it like locomotive steam. "I may have an entirely new outlook on your lifestyle after this."

Her sigh turns into a cough. "Afraid ah might too."

My ears perk up. Our voices sound different now; the acoustics of the room have changed. I peer up to see an opening has been revealed in the ceiling, around the notched pole. A single flap of my wings carries me over the ornate copper shell. My toes and wing fingers grip the beam and allow its use as a ladder. With due care, I climb onto the top of the tortoise shell. A short climb sees me up the pole and into some new space. After checking the floor for further traps, I climb in. Columns of light pierce the darkness, resting upon various new tortoise engravings.

Below me, commotion rises. "Move outta the way, lawbat." She moves to stomp her way up onto the artifact.

"Don't climb on the shell!"

"Why?" Her ears launch up like signal flags. "Thing had no objections to clamping down on me."

I sigh. "It is clearly an objet d'art."

Wariness cools her enthusiasm. Her boot returns, gingerly, to the floor.

I must admit I'm impressed with her regard for the arts. "Toss me the rope and I'll pull you up. You can brace against this pole without wrecking the shell."

With wary slowness, she shrugs the rope off her shoulders and throws it to me. Once I secure it, she hops clear of the shell and starts walking up the notched pole. "So help me, Blake, if ah wind up with a tail full a' darts…"

With a resigned groan, I decide correcting her now would only increase the odds off her damaging the massive shell. Instead, I offer a wing and pull her the rest of the way up. Together we stand and take account of the room.

About half the size of the one below it, the space is again round and circled by a band of carvings in the stone. A spiral of air shafts streams light around to various points of the chamber, illuminating specific portions of the wall. On a pedestal at the center of the room gleams a turtle figurine, about an inch tall.

She searches around the room for some hidden passage or compartment. "Where's the great treasure?"

"I think that is your great treasure." I lift a wing at the stone pedestal at the center of the room.

She glances askew at it, then kneels to examine it closer. Its copper shell looks quite a bit like the giant on that trapped her minutes before. "We came through all that for this little bug?"

"It makes some sense. The tribe that built this wanted you to learn patience. Giving you a huge reward wouldn't seem their style." Without being as obvious as her, I search the room for any more loose stonework. "It might even be token, meant to be retrieved as a sort of test."

A scowl darkens her muzzle. "Testin' mah patience, all right."

I pad up next to her. "I think it's rather darling."

"Ah'm sure ya do." Her blue eyes roll, catching the light with a sapphire gleam. "Yer keen on fine little things."

"I am." I stretch up and kiss her cheek.

"Don't go butterin' me up now." She crosses her arms at me. "Ah've still got mah dander up over this nonsense."

We depart the complex at a more assured pace than we entered. The occasional copper snapper clattering at our heels only winds Six up further. At long last, I walk with her out of the tunnel and into the warm sunlight of an Arizona afternoon. "I have to admit, Six: that was quite pleasant."

"Tribe that dug this thing's lucky they vanished, or ah'd give 'em a piece of mah mind." She shoves the little tortoise into my grasp.

I study the bauble, having not noticed her snatch it in the first place. "You don't want to keep it? I'm sure it'd worth something to a collector of antiquities."

The mention of money raises her eyebrows, but she heaved a deep sigh. "No... You keep it. Ah'd rather have you happy than some rich dunce."

We head back into the buttes and twisty cliffsides and begin the long climb that will lead us back toward White Rock.

Chapter 2

I reckon all his fun parts run pink.

Light floods out the opening door. The sheriff strides up all doleful, wings folded, his gold-flecked eyes on the stars.

I lay a paw on his shoulder.

Being grabbed by shadows startles him some. Goes for his gun, but I pluck it from his grasp. Being the clever sort, he bowls into me, knocking us both to the dirt.

Pinning him to the gravel before he can fuss further, I smile, panting. "This ain't exactly the sort of tumble ah was aiming for, sugar bat."

He stutters like a seizing telegrapher. "S-Si—"

I lay a finger on his lips, returning the iron I lightened him of.

He fumbles it into his holster with one hind paw, staring up at me. Looks awful darling like that, all startled and joyful in the moonlight; not my fault I need to kiss him for it. He relaxes under me a moment, then breaks off to glance into the night. Nobody's around, but I let him up, figuring we've got better things to do than lay in the gravel all night. I've no sooner dusted off my clothes than he's herding me into the City Office on his wing. Eager little thing.

A swift boot shuts the door, and I'm alone with my lawbat. Silver light plays along the coal-black fuzz of his wings. A lonesome longing burns inside me as I recall how silky it feels against my nose, my tongue, my...

"I thought you left." He's fixing to sound tough— if he wore boots, though, he'd be shaking in them.

"Turned around." And, even with a price still on my head, he ought to know better. "Figured one more night in your company wouldn't go amiss."

"You're welcome to all the nights you want." His wing fingers close on my paw. "Days too."

I slip a paw along his muzzle, all gentle-like. "I don't put up fences, I just ride 'em. This is just the way of the world right now."

Before he can get another word out, I kiss him again. He lifts up to meet it, obliging my paws to run up his back.

He breathes real deep, then manages to pull away from my kiss again. "You're in heat."

Bashfulness sweeps through my ears, but fails to stop my nibbling along the bottom of his muzzle. I've always been the willful sort.

Hushed by my bunny charms, the sheriff folds his wings around me. I rest my muzzle on his, feeling all secure and longed for. Matter of fact, I'm feeling quite a bit of longing pressed against my more private regions. I press right back, eliciting a tender eep from the fruit bat.

Giggling like a fool, I throw the lawbat over my shoulder. He agitates some as I carry him down the hall to his room, putting on a show of trying to squirm free, but I keep hold. He has a cozy little bedroom. Some might take it as being a mite small, but it's got plenty of room for what I'm planning to do with him. Even just walking feels all slick and tingly. I set the sheriff down, thunder rumbling through my heartbeat. My eyes settle on the tidy little bed. "Sleepin' up in the rafters still?"

A blush creeps into his voice. "When you're not here, Six, I'm upside down in more ways than one."

I blush too, hiding behind my ears as I settle in next to him. "That ain't fair. Nothing ah say ever sounds like that."

He brushes my ears aside, cradling my cheek. "Maybe not to you…"

Darn lawbat keeps compelling me to kiss him. This time I get brave and lick on his lips some. Shouldn't surprise him— he's the only fella I practice such skills with, and he knows I'm real fond of when he does tricks with that twister of a tongue he's got. His wing thumbs trace through my chest fluff, over my galloping heart and down the buttons of my vest.

Clothes fall to the floor as we get to gettin' reacquainted. Soon I'm wearing nothing but a gunbelt and straddling the sheriff. His soft wings caress my back; his brown eyes glimmer up at mine, with more gold than most river prospectors see in a lifetime. I want to ask him if he loves me, but am fearful of any answers he might give. Instead, I ease myself down onto the warmth of his body, letting it soothe away all those cold desert nights.

Erect and hot, he feels right pleasant against my fur. I angle up, rubbing my lips along its length. Blake moans, then giggles.

I cross my arms over my naked breasts. Blazes, do my nipples feel tender and hard. "Just what are you gigglin' at, sheriff?"

"Your tail! It's tickling my... my..."

I glance back, then bob my fluffy tail against his sac. He squirms, arching his body up against me. I show mercy and let him pull me down for a kiss. After a few fluttery touches of our muzzles, he turns his head a little, allowing himself better access to my mouth. The taste of canned peaches lingers on his breath. That long, talented tongue coils around mine, milking it. Feels mighty unusual, even if he did use it on me a while back. Granted, he used it elsewhere...

I carry on rubbing against his length, spreading slick wetness as I ride. My poor little bunny burrow clenches for attention. Reaching down, I lift the head of his member and prod it against my opening. Takes a little wrangling, and a moment passes where I question my technique, but then I gasp as he spreads me wide.

Blake gives joyful little squeaks as I work my way down onto him. Doesn't hurt like I recall, but the going in is powerful tight. I try to set my loins at ease—this was their idea, after all. I grope at the base of his shaft, feeling that he's about halfway into me. Trembling at the thought, I press on, my pale ears swaying down to his dark-furred chest. In the moonlight, the black tips of them seem to be picking up his color.

It's a peculiar thing, making love for the second time and without a recently relocated shoulder. Allows a bunny to notice the little things. Like how she can feel the pulse of his heartbeat as he's buried inside her.

I lift off him a ways, mouth opening in a breathless sigh at the empty feeling this brings. Not that I mind how it tugs on my nethers, mind you. Letting my weight carry me back down, I slip onto him again. I tilt my head and watch in the moonlight as our fur meets. I keep thrusting and try a few different angles, seeing what feels best. I find that laying down close to him feels mighty pleasant, allowing my clit to rub right into his fur, and still affords me plenty of room to bounce like I'm standing in the stirrups.

My gunbelt catches on the fur of Blake's belly, drawing forth a pitiable whimper. "Oww!"

"Sorry, Jordan." I hold stone-still. My clit tingles in the chill night air. "Didn't mean to."

"I'm okay." He rubs where I pulled his fur, then caresses my shoulders with his wing thumbs. I can hear a smile in his panted breath. "Don't stop on my account."

I hitch the gunbelt higher, so as not to repeat the performance. On powerful bunny legs, I bounce up and down his shaft. Feels awful nice to be the one doing the riding. We've only done it once before, and I was in no condition to be on top. Feels awful nice in general, having that healthy length of lawbat inside me. The sheriff starts humping back, move in time with me as much as my clumsy thrusts allow. Doesn't seem to bother him none, judging by how he cups my modest breasts, squeezing all tender-like, letting my nipple rub against his palms. Ain't my most sensitive bits, compared with elsewhere, though I'm glad he's keen on them, since nobody else notices 'em. Blake, though, he gives a little extra twitch down below, swelling a little more against me. Makes a bunny blush, seeing how he fancies them so.

I do some squeezing of my own, picking up speed. Blake's gasping for air. Breath, his and mine, sways my ears. Lewd squishing resounds through the little room. I'm riding at full tilt now, slamming down so hard I feel his sac bounce. So hard the bed squeaks. Lawbat squeaks too, muzzle open, teeth glinting silver in the moonbeams, hunching against me like a bat possessed. Bucking hard inside me, his penis swelling just a touch wider. Wing thumbs grab my hips. Squeaks run to gasps, gasps to a breathless stammer. Then he starts spraying ropes of seed against my tender walls. I shudder, feeling pulses of heat and pressure spread down his member.

In his fit, he pinches on my nipples, causing me to jerk down against him out of reflex. My sore little clit grinds against the base of his pulsing erection, driving pleasure through my body in lightning strikes. My paw flashes down to give it a proper rub. Doesn't take much before pleasure's overwhelming me fast, what with the flatter of the lawbat's enjoyment of me. I clench hard on the spurting shaft within me, the muscles of my vagina dancing all frantic, milking my sweet fruit bat for all he's worth.

When the world returns from being a haze of pleasure, I find myself muzzle to muzzle with the sheriff. I clutch him tighter than all that's dear in this world, reveling in the silky warmth he brings, inside and out. Buried in me, wrapped around me, I feel all full and cared for. I fall into dreams with a blanket against the night, wrapped up in my fella's wings. "Jordan... Oh, Jordan..."

↓ ↯ ↓

I wake to birds chittering, warm sun, and a pretty little lawbat in my arms. Seems he's still asleep. I lie there and to myself, burying my worries in the soft of his fur. After a spell, I get to feeling the need for some diversion, my claws tracing down his chest fluff. This path leads me under the covers for a little prospecting. His fur runs coffee-brown, though his chest has more orange. His smooth midriff lead my paws down along where his wings connect, then onward to his muscled legs and tight little rump. Silky fur whispers through mine, touching me like only the wind does.

Blame my heat, blame my bunny ways, but I'm feeling more a woman than a lady. Under the glow of the blankets, I uncover what Blake looks like when I'm not driving him to distraction.

Seems I'm quite the wild hare when nobody can see, because all of a sudden the lawbat's getting some awful familiar nuzzles. I nibble on his sheath with my lips, tugging at the soft chewiness. My nose twitches at his scent: male, musky, inviting. Warm too, and growing warmer. My paw closes in around the base of his length. Still nuzzling in on his equipment, I start rubbing up and down his hidden shaft. As I stroke, I can feel him growing in my paw. Front of the sheath's still nice and loose, so when I pull it back the pink tip peeks out, then gets covered again. Amuses me that it's pink, when all the rest of him runs coffee-brown. Well, except his tongue; I reckon all his fun parts run pink.

After playing with him a spell, he firms up and pokes right on out of the sheath on his own. The head's peeking out, so I get real brave and lick on that too. Same fruity taste greets me, wonders where I've been for so long. His skin's still got a little slack, so I keep rubbing as I taste him.

I'd never have thought I'd take to this so, but feeling him grow on my tongue feels unusual and grand. Then again, most things about fellas seem unusual and grand.

The sheriff moans and rolls to his back as I tongue around his sheath. Not overly sure about what I'm doing here, but the stiff length of lawbat in my paw insists I've got a handle on matters. Sets a real bounce to a bunny's tail, if you take my meaning.

Blake draws the blanket back. We meet eyes. Still tonguing to beat the band, I let my nose twitch against the underside of his tip.

Passion sets a gleam to the grin of my polite little lawbat.

I squeak a giggle and let Blake drag me up his body. That hot length blazes a trail between my breasts, down my stomach, and against my heat-addled lady bits. My thin-furred loins grow damp as I ride the underside of his length. He's real stiff now, balls moving whenever I rub up on his sheath. Having heard that can be a tender area on fellas, I scoot up and wiggle atop his round tip for a while. Softer than the shaft. Could be that it's hotter too—but then that could be me. I remember to lift up my gunbelt so as not to jab the poor fella again. A wing reaches up to caress my breast. I smile and ride harder.

We continue riding along for a spell. Each thrust rubs my little clitty against his tip and belly fur. Each frantic gasp from Blake stokes the furnace of my heat. Warmth builds in me like a kindled fire, blazing higher and higher, burning up my thoughts of anything else as I buck against the right-lovely texture of his shaft.

I freeze, a hare's breath from going over the edge.

My body quivers atop him, taut and tense.

Velvet wings pull me close.

I go off.

"Aa! Aa! Aaaaaahhh!" I bury my face between his shoulder and pillow, hollering with pleasure as my body floods with trembles centering on my nethers, on the delightful cock wedged against them, leaving me gasping 'til I'm breathless and shuddering with aftershocks. My hips press hard on him, my legs squeezing on him like a skittish pony—meanwhile other parts of me make it known they'd like something to squeeze on too. I grip his shoulders. He holds me against his wiry frame. Fluffy and soft, breathing hard, stiff against me: Blake's a whole mess of feeling. I try to tell him how nice he feels, but I only manage "Oh...oh... Jordan... Hah..." over the hammering beat of my heart.

A true gentleman, Blake waits real patient-like while I recuperate. Tender wings stroke down my back. Sappy words breeze past my ears. Sticky juices make our fur a ticklish mess. Feels right pleasant and I tell him so.

He chuckles against me. "You, madam, have got quite a way of saying good morning."

I grope for something clever, but my brains've turned to jelly. Instead, I roll us to our sides. Feeling a heavy slickness between my legs, I reach down and scout the area. My paw comes back slick and damp. "Glad sakes, Jordan. Look how wet ya made me!"

The fruit bat blushes scarlet under his chocolate fur, sputtering. "S-Six!"

I kiss him on the nose and grab his penis with my wet paw. "Way you look at me, lawbat, yer gonna get rode hard and put away wet now an' then."

"That's—uh!—hardly a ladylike thing to..." Poor Blake. Talking ain't his strong suit once I start rubbing him against my tingling lips.

I breathe into his ears, whispering soft and rubbing hard. "Forget ladylike—I think you know what this bunny'd like..."

Riled and ready, Blake bucks against me, and it takes a few tries to line him up proper. Once I do, he thrusts halfway up into me at a shot, squeezing the air from my lungs. I drape a leg over his hip, right where his wing joins the rest of him, and pull in a welcoming way.

We set to doing what bunnies do.

He's deep and thrusting shallow, pumping my foolishly damp passage 'til I can hear each in and out. His sac bumps against my thigh as he drives himself in to the hilt once more. His breath washes hot against my neck, like a desert breeze. Laying side-by-side, his thrusts rub on different parts of my passage than before. He nuzzles into my chest fluff.

My muzzle curls in a smile. My ears droop, the window's light glows pink through them at the edge of my vision. My modest breasts jiggle each time he buries himself in me, and, if I time it right, I can clench on him as he's sliding out. Lawbat sure takes to that, breathing hard as he works into me.

At some point in our little hoedown, the pillow jostles from under his head, leaving his neck at a funny angle. I slide my arm in as a replacement, since that seems the polite thing to do, what with him making cute little grunts and groans as he drives jolts of joy through my body.

I lay back and let him do the work. He gets frantic, unsteady in his motions, 'til at last I feel his length swell inside me, then spurt out blast after blast of his silky seed. His teeth set, glinting in the fiery light of dawn. Those gold-flecked eyes shut as he loses himself in the moment. Delicate gushes of warmth cause my muscles to spasm in time with him. My eyes squeeze shut in delight, but stop neither morning light nor tingling pleasure. I hold him holstered, now that he's done going off. His body slackens against me. Whenever he moves, his softening length slicks against every bump and valley of my walls. I giggle like a fool. My body's too heavy to move, my heart too light to keep from pulsing wonder through me. I just lie, warmed by sunlight and fruit bat juices. We breathe together. Even with my heat satisfied for the moment, I know I'd be powerful lonesome without him.

Cuddling up, we pay no heed to the sticky mess in our fur. He kisses his way up and down my ears. I'm awful ticklish on the pink insides, so I wind up laughing into a pillow as he nuzzles without mercy.

"Glory be, lawbat." I flop to my back, my arm still behind his head. "Ya act like you never thought to see me again."

He looks to me, all soulful. "I didn't."

Ears drooping all coy-like, I kiss him on his little foxy nose. "You're a fool."

"Stay."

"Can't."

Blake touches my shoulder like I'm made of fine china. "I'd hate to see you hurt again."

"Don't need to worry about me, Jordan." I wiggle up naked against him and nuzzle my twitching nose in his fluff. "I'm the tough sort."

His wing thumbs cup my muzzle, bringing me level with gold constellations in the dark of his eyes, with all the hope I light in them. "How about one day, Six? One day."

Seeing as how my brain's gone as fuzzy as Blake's whole body, I just giggle an "alright" like the fool I am.

"Come on, lawbat! Don't ya want yer trousers back?"

"I need those! Six, this isn't—- The washer-woman has my other pairs!" A quick wing snatches at them. I'm quicker.

Clothed and decent, I bounce around the room keeping Blake separated from his garments. "And here ah reckoned you had life all planned out. One little bunny razes it all to ruin."

Another miss. The boy'd be better at this game if he wasn't so concerned with keeping a wing over his nakedness. He scowls. "One bunny is all I can abide."

"So you're a one-bunny bat?" Trousers balled up behind my back, I lean down for a kiss.

The pretty fruit bat's ears drop. "By now, you ought to know what sort of man I am." His soft lips meet mine.

I let the kiss linger for a spell, then smile at him. "The sort without any trousers!" I go bouncing down the hall, pants in paw.

The sheriff stifles a cuss, pauses for a thought, then comes chasing after me. We giggle and raise ruckus down the hall. After much grabbing and wrestling, the lawbat makes a bold dive, almost flying, pinning me to the sitting room floor. Wicked thoughts cross my bunny mind about what we might get to out here.

I pant under his scrawny body, his fur and breath soft against me. Some intimate twitches bring a blush to my ears. "Why Mister Blake, you'll just take any opportunity to get atop me, won't ya?"

He opens his muzzle to say something clever, but I seize two pawfuls of his bare rump. He makes all manner of cute batty noises, then tenses above me, staring and stunned.

I follow his gaze to a surprised and, from where I'm laying, upside-down canine.

"Well, good morning, Deputy Harding." I tip the hat I'm not wearing in salute.

After a pause, the old bloodhound raises his teacup in return. "Morning."

My lawbat scandalized, I'm left alone with the deputy, who is showing me an entirely different brand of hospitality. Sipping on a glass of cool peach tea, I wonder just how he brews it. Must chill the tea somehow after steepin' it, then mix in peach preserves without making it thick on the tongue.

I tip my hat to the hound. "Mah apologies about the little show you got, Harding."

"Don't worry on it." He shakes his droopy muzzle. "Though it'd pay for the two a' yew to be more cautious."

"Were the lawbat any more cautious, we'd never get him down from the rafters." My paws curl around the cool sides of the teacup.

The old dog busies himself pouring another cup. "I'm willin' to bet you could."

I drown my shyness in a sip. "Some mighty fine tea you brewed me."

"My mama's recipe." Under all that bloodhound sadness, he smiles. "Hurts Blake something terrible, how you keep leavin'."

I take a seat opposite Harding in the sitting room, watching the dust dance in the morning sun. "Doesn't do me any wonders either."

Before the dog can respond, Blake ambles back in a state of dress. Bat doesn't meet either of our eyes as he glances out the window. "Any news, Deputy?"

"Nothin' especially. Got the postal stagecoach comin' through today. Gotta watch out for those quiet days though. Tea?"

"I'm not in a mood for sitting down just now."

I stifle a laugh. I'll have to see about his mood when we get a moment. "You goin' on patrol, lawbat?"

"It's my turn. Though with you here…" He manages to shoot me a grin.

"Hey now! I don't mean to leave the bloodhound in a jam on account of mah sticking around for a day."

"A consideration you seem to lack with me."

"Ya don't seem to mind terribly the jams I put you in." I kick my feet up on an empty chair and smile all sweet-like.

Blake fights down a fluster, crossing his wings. "What do you propose?"

"I'll tag along on patrol. Keep mahself outta trouble while we go around keepin' folk from having a good time." That should suit his fancy.

"I suppose I could deputize you for the day."

"Deputy nothin'! I'm not fixing to be your lackey. No offense, Harding."

The deputy shrugs and takes another gulp of peach tea.

Lawbat lifts his ears at me. "Six, if you're not a deputy, you'll have to stay out of the way should anything happen." His muzzle dips with a smile. "You really think you can do that?"

I settle my arms behind my head, leaning the chair back. "Reckon you'll just have to make me sheriff too, then."

"...Alright."

The chair bucks wild under me. I about spill onto the floor. "Whoa! Say what now?"

"Nothing in the city charter sets a limit of just one sheriff. You can be one." Those pretty brown eyes narrow on me. "Only for today, mind you."

"I'll be needin' a badge."

He gets a smart little smirk. "That's the easy part."

As Harding looks on, amused, Blake offers me a wing. I take it and rise, following him into the office. Once inside, the sheriff opens a file cabinet and slides the papers back to reveal a strongbox affixed inside. Keys jingle from his belt to his wing thumbs, unlocking it. He takes out an old silver sheriff's badge.

"That belonged to my uncle." He pins it on my vest, then flips something shinier out of the box. "And I believe this belongs to you."

I take the pin, turning it over in my paws. "And here ah'd thought you'd do somethin' all romantic like wear it 'til I came back."

He touches my arm. "Some things I'm not willing to risk losing."

That sets a real blush to my ears. I glance away, at the strongbox. Has some cash in it, maybe a hundred in a neat stack of greenbacks, along with some old journals and a sack of coins. I affix the pin to its usual home, if displaced a bit by the sheriff star. "What now?"

Blake slips on his hat and tips it my way. "Now we walk through town on my route, and keep folks from having a good time."

⩗ ⩜ ⩗

"Took down those wanted posters of you."

"Much obliged."

Blake looks at me looking at folk who look at me. "With Hayes gone, everybody ought to realize there's no reward to be had."

"Seein' as how they gotta turn me in to you, daresay ah could make my escape easy enough." I wink his way.

"Let's see it doesn't come to that." His wing brushes against me. Would like to have him on my arm, though I got enough eyes my way at present. I settle for walking close to him.

We see to sifting the heap of humdrum the bat's so keen on. Ferret kits tussle and steal a ball of string from each other. More lawsome folk busy themselves with their shops and shopping. Some saddlery horse compliments me on my new gunbelt; neither Blake nor I return his wink. The lawbat later confides to me that he had the thing commissioned at his tack shop.

Being all peaceable bores me some, though talking to the lawbat is a mite nicer than I'll admit to him. Besides, we've got more hats tipping our way than a windstorm.

"Funny how everybody around you makes a point a' being all law-abiding."

His pearly whites shine a smile my way. "Yourself included."

I shoot him a dark glance from the shade of my hat. "Ah'd take it as a kindness if you didn't remind me."

His wing rises to pat me on the shoulder, but just like that I feel a tug from my gun. Both paws slip to my belt, feeling the gun that's there and the one I need to beat out of the lion Hayes. The pull of their echo, gentle but insisting, diverts me to the saloon.

"Six, isn't it a bit early for drinking?" He follows.

"A mite, yes." I breeze in the doors.

Musk and cheap whiskey hang like whore's tits—still obvious, but covered up a trifle for the late morning crowd. Patrons trickle back in, or never left, sitting all bleary at the tables. The main topic of debate seems to be if they should go across the street to eat lunch or stay here and drink it. I recognize two mutts playing dominos, but they're regulars.

Light glints through the barkeep's prized collection of colorful bottles. Dusts them more often than the windows, it seems. A collie with a lazy ear, he trots behind the bar, tending his flock of firewater and rotgut. His daughter's around, always is. Nice enough gal, sheepish for a collie; pity her position as a saloon girl keeps most folk looking down their muzzles at her.

The cat at the piano has either been tipped too much or not enough, so he yowls into a bawdy tune about an armadillo from Amarillo. Nothing to write home about, but I'm impressed he can rhyme so many words to "bordello." Blake goes a little pink in the ears. Maybe the song's not so bad after all.

We stand off to one side, just taking in the scene. Waiting to see why the echo in my gun yanked me so.

In the corner, a 'dillo in a poncho unrolls from his slump over the bar, bleary-eyed. He rises from his puddle of drool and profanity. By the width of his ears and the narrow of his eyes, I'd hazard he's a little pinch hung-over.

The piano cat continues his shrill caterwaul, until a coffin varnish bottle comes hurtling against his piano, no doubt aimed at his head.

"Ah take exception tah yer song, fleabag." The 'dillo's nose wiggles in fury, claws smacking against the floor. "Ah won't abide no slurs against my kin."

The cat hisses up from nursing the fresh dent in his piano. His white tail spikes out like a bottlebrush. "I'll play whatever tickles my fancy!"

Claws glint in the dim room. On any other day, he'd be a bad sport for that, but armadillos aren't known for responding to the customary exchange of wallops. Wells Fargo hires them by the score because they bring their own armor.

The mutts pause their game of dominos, turning to watch as they cheat each other.

Blake steps forward, but I touch his slim shoulder.

I meet his pretty eyes. "Let me handle this one, lawbat."

He gets a contrary look, but sighs. His wing sweeps me onward.

Two strides and I grip the 'dillo's back armor. The bumpy texture uneases my paws as I hold him back. I could lighten his pockets, and probably ought to, but I refrain for the lawbat's sake. "What seems to be the trouble, friend?"

"Who in the hell are you?" Beady, half-hazed eyes glare up at me.

I give my badge a little shine. "Ah'm the sheriff."

Around the saloon, eyes and ears turn to Blake. I take the moment to scoot a table closer to the 'dillo.

The lawbat shrugs. "Provisionally, yes."

My small armored pal puffs himself up, plates shifting, though he's not even up to my chest. All self-important, spits on my boots.

I drive two fingers against his chest. Beady eyes spring wide. Slowly, slowly, he tips. His toes lift off the floor. Rolls from tail to rump to back. His puny arms flail at nothing.

I kick a second table against him, wedging the drunk 'dillo in place. "Ease off, roly-poly."

The domino mutts bark a laugh each. The collie barkeep hides his grinning muzzle. His daughter points her long nose to the back room.

I spare a quick look at Blake, but he's leaning back against the bar, content to superintend from a ways off.

"Now you." I turn to the piano cat.

He squirms as I loom over him like the noonday sun. "Me?"

"Ah think it's time to change yer tune."

I weigh down his tip jar with a silver dollar, then whisper in his pointy ear. I step back, trading a look with Blake, as the piano player settles into his seat, cracks his paws, and sets to tickling ivory.

"Don't think this settles things!" The 'dillo snaps at my heels as I stride past.

"That any way to talk to a fella buying you drinks?" I flip a coin onto the bar. Barkeep jiggers me two hurried shots.

I set both drinks beside the 'dillo, who offers a somewhat less sour expression. I cross my arms, trying to sound like Blake, only manly. "Now, if we're reasonable fellas, this'll be the part where you have a couple drinks and wait for somebody to move these tables." I place a paw on the heavy wood.

His horsey ears swivel back, but his voice has lost its edge. "And if we ain't?"

"Then I tie your nose to your tail and roll you down Skull Creek Gulch." I smile down at him. "Comprende?"

A grumble of agreement.

"Glad to see you're a good sport after all." I resist the urge to goad him. Much. Blake follows me out of the saloon as the cat mewls into the chorus of "My Flabby Tabby Mistress."

⤋ ⚡ ⤋

"Handled that well." His wing rests on my shoulder as we walk onto the porch of the City Office. Street's empty. Sand and heat are the only things that linger this time of day. His gold eyes glint at me. "Though a trifle unorthodox."

Ears up, chest out, I wiggle the paw that picked my own pocket. "I fancied it up for your sake."

His wing thumbs squeeze my shoulder. "Have you given any thought to becoming a real deputy?"

I tug down the brim of my hat, using my whiskey voice. "You given any thought to a life a' crime?"

"Touché."

"Stop makin' up words, sheriff." I shake my head. "Nobody understands what yer sayin'."

"That's a perfectly valid— Oh."

I smile, all sweet-like.

His ears flatten. "If I wanted sass, I have foxes aplenty."

"And not a one like me."

A frown sours his fruit bat muzzle. "Don't I know it..."

The door creaks open, letting out a gust of bloodhound.

"Deputy?"

"Howdy, Sheriff." A slow nod, then the dog jostles a beaded bag onto his shoulder. "Reckon I'll head off for the evenin'. Got some business with the 'yotes tonight."

"Oh?" Blake scratches an ear, baffled in the noonday sun. "I didn't remember you mentioning..."

"Came up sudden-like."

I smile. "Think you'd better give the hound his leave, Sheriff. In fact, as sheriff myself, I order him to go. For the sake a' the town."

"Six, you're only sheriff provis—"

"Alright, then. Ah may be late in the mornin' too, just so you're aware." He tips his hat. "You folks have a right pleasant night."

The dog and I trade conspiring glances, then he shuffles down the road with the slightest of wags. Dust swirls after his steps in pale puffs, the air rippling with heat.

Blake squints after his deputy. For a bat, he doesn't seem to mind the day. Has a couple hats, but he tends to lose them—what with his habit of flying and all. "Harding's not the type to just take off like that."

"Well…" My paw closes on his vest, dragging him inside the office. I shut the door after him, in case any prying eyes do brave this heat. "Let me show ya the type ah am…" In the cool shadows, I drop my ears and gaze down at my lawbat.

A nervous chuckle. "Right in the middle of the day?" He nuzzles the tip of one ear, then the other.

I breathe into his ear, hoping he'll take to that. I always do. "Sun ain't the only heat you'd better mind today."

He gets on his tiptoes and kisses me. "Your radiance, madam, outshines it a thousandfold."

I haven't the first clue on what to say to that, so I kiss him back. My arms wrap him up, paws surveying up his wings, under his vest, along his back. All the while, his tongue's dancing across and around mine, robbing me of my wits. We're soon leaning against the wall, muzzle to muzzle, hip to hip. Being taller, I bend my knees a little to hunch against him, obliged as I am to the tingle between my thighs.

Breaking the kiss, he nestles his head under my chin. His wings rub the curve of my muscled bunny rump, groping on my fluffy tail.

I keep up my soft thrusts. "Yer sure panting, lawbat." My paws slide down the front of his vest, undoing buttons all the way. "We'd best get you outta these clothes."

His ears dip, shy-like. "Right here?"

"Reckon this is a fine place." I flash him a grin and bury my paws in his trousers.

The consternation in his eyes fades like stars at dawn, outshone by pleasure as I jerk the loose skin of his sheath. His naked flesh runs smooth, hot, silky in my paws. He moans. Sometime around my stroking down to his sac, his trousers run short of room, so I do the polite thing and undo his fly. In what's becoming a familiar and welcome sight, his pink shaft meets the daylight, still mostly hidden in its chocolate sheath. I stroke the sheath with one paw, teasing at the emerging head with the other. He shudders and, about halfway stiff, he melts like butter against me.

After a spell, I figure this'll be easier from my knees. From down here, his scent runs richer, closer. I feel a rush of nerves and delight at the scandalous moment we're in, the state I can put an upstanding lawbat into with just a touch of my paws. I can feel his heartbeat along the smooth skin of his cock.

He's hard now, his sheath stretched somewhat taut around the shaft. I used to think it looked like a pony's, but, upon further examination, his looks far prettier. More delicate. Matches the rest of him. I rub it against the soft fur of my cheek.

Blake gasps.

"Good?" I look up, cradling him with care in both paws.

His voice fades to a murmur even as his eyes glimmer down on me. "Yes."

"Good." I notice a glimmer of liquid at his tip and kiss it away. He fancies most things I do to him, but I was a tad rough on him the first time, so I still like to watch his face to be sure. What's more, it's an interesting angle to have on the lawbat: one of the rare moments he can look down to me. I kiss down the folds of his sheath, then back to his tip, all the while meeting his eyes. Heat rises in my ears, though, and my gaze shifts to the task at hand.

I stroke the sheriff faster, my fingertips skimming over the surface. Now and again, I let my paws do their reloading tricks on his tip, though I know this weapon's already loaded.

"Mmmmmm, Six…" His wing cups my cheek. "H-hold on a minute."

I watch him, wondering if I did something or didn't.

He steps sideways, and I let him slip from my grasp, then let him take my paw. "Come on. I want to show you something."

We scamper back to his bedroom. Good thing he had my paw; I'm liable to run into a wall with his pink shaft bobbing around like that.

"You may need to..." His ears drop as he grapples with stammers. "Your trousers might interfere."

I can't say shucking my pants with Blake sounds like a bad idea, so I kick out of my boots, then slide off everything below my gunbelt.

Blake hops, hooks his wing thumbs into the rafter, then flips over so he's dangling from his hind paws. His cock sways at eye level. Looks at me as if that's normal. "Sit down on the bed."

"Ah see what yer up to, lawbat." I bounce onto the mattress, only to find, for the first time since I hit my head on a fox's doorway, that I'm not tall enough. I can lick the tip of his member, but I'll have to bounce up to lick the shaft. I stick out my tongue, balancing him on it for a moment, then happen upon an idea. Inspired, I grab both his pillows, stack them, and plant my fluffy tail on top.

I turn and get a spot more of his slickness on my nose, which twitches at the heat-then-cool of it. Blake smiles up at me from my lap and grips my tail. I giggle and wipe the fluid away, though his musk clings close, riling me something fierce. I start stroking on my lawbat, who's only softened a little from our new arrangement. I lick up the side, tonguing the soft folds of his sheath—

I squeak.

With a mischievous look, Blake's tilted his head sideways and against my slit. His pretty muzzle finds its way between my legs. Kisses and licks run from my clit downward, causing me to shift my legs wider. His breath breezes hot through my fur. His tongue dances over my naked lips, then darts into me, drawing nectar from what I can assure is a juicy area.

Then he sets his lips to me and begins working me over like the tastiest peach in Georgia. Every now and then, his tongue flicks, like he's clucking it. I tense and twitch through a couple before I realize what they are; guess my cave is worthy of a few echomahwhatsits too. The thought clenches my passage, even as his tongue wiggles ever deeper into me.

With all the commotion in my loins, seems I've forgotten my end of the deal. I get back to stroking him. I take his tip into my mouth real gentle-like, giving clumsy licks to that elegant, naked pommel of flesh. Meanwhile, his balls bounce against the top of my paw as I jerk his tight sheath, warm and velvet-soft.

His body tenses against me as he starts licking with desperate eagerness.

The rafter creaks as his feet dig into it. His cock swells in my mouth.

I tremble, a hare's breath from going off, giving a frantic suckle.

The first gush of salty bat seed sprays my tongue.

I squeal around his cock, clutching him close.

Another gush—thick and sweet—spilling out.

His tongue whips, clit to depths, wild.

Hot seed races down my cheek.

My feet beat on the floor.

Thighs tighten on him.

Eyes roll back.

"Jordan!"

I plummet into orgasm, thrusting rapid-fire against his muzzle, my entire passage clenching on his dancing tongue, needing him ever deeper, ever closer, ever in my arms, no matter how big of fools we are, I can't help but holler as the passion rises through me like my whole soul's blooming into being. He sprays another spurt, which lands on my breasts, though by the sound his lips are making against mine, I'm giving him a run for his money. My toes curl and I'm aware of the fur between them getting flattened, just as I'm aware of the softness of the pillows and the desperately true feeling of having him in my arms. A few more clenches and I'm spent, shuddering in aftershocks. His breath tingles against my tender lips. Light-headed, I feel the world start to tip forward, but Jordan's there to catch me and ease me down with his wings.

On my back, I pant up at him. Still on the rafter, the last drips of his semen fall on my thighs. He's swinging front to back, no doubt from my wild movements. I reach up. He swings forward and takes my paw. We stay like that for a moment, fingers woven with wing thumbs, then I nod to the empty half of the bed. He smiles and slips from the rafter and into my arms.

Sun's lower now, and the heat's died down. My muzzle traces up his naked chest. Here I am: back in bed, middle of the afternoon, and not complaining.

He rolls to one side and pulls something from his nightstand. "I've been saving these for a special occasion." The tin shines in his wing thumbs. "I'd say this constitutes one." He wrestles with the tin some, but, just as I reach to do it for him, the top pops open.

A wondrous scent blooms forth. Exotic and familiar, it draws me back to another life, one I crossed a country to escape.

I take one of the little dark chunks. Pressed into little bricks, they're just the least bit tacky from heat. My fur sticks as if it knows how much I want them. "Genuine dates?"

"Yes, ma'am." He perks up with pride. "From Arabia and everything."

Holding it in my claws, I wiggle my nose closer to the sweet scent. "How'd you lay wing on them?"

"My aunt mailed them here for Yuletide." His fluffy chest puffs with pride.

I chuckle on the notion of a whole family of lawbats divvying up perfect, law-abiding slices of fruitcake. "That was right thoughtful a' her." I sneak another morsel from the tin, holding it up to the light so the little bits of sugar twinkle. I put a little bite into it and the smile I give to Blake. "She know you're sharin' 'em with a tall, trousered bunny in bed?"

His kiss breezes gentle across my lips. "I could introduce you."

I eat the rest of the date, letting the syrupy results mingle with the lingering taste of Blake. "Awful good, lawbat. You gonna make me finish 'em all by mah lonesome?"

His wing drapes over my hip. "Maybe I wanted the sweetest thing from one desert to try the sweetest from another."

"Maybe ah'm sweet enough already." I pluck another one from the tin, using my claws so as not to get my white fur dirty. Grandma'd be pleased by my etiquette, though maybe not by my being in and out of trousers all day. I drag the date across Blake's lips, all teasing-like.

That talented tongue snakes out from his grin, plucking the date from between my fingers. I giggle as he kisses the sugar from my fur.

The lawbat cottons to my idea, it seems. All grace and care, he's pulling another date from the tin. The smell wiggles my nose. Opening my muzzle, I let him place it on my tongue. Tastes sweet as sugar, but feels dry as desert. I reach for my canteen—a bunny needs more than sweetness to get by. Yet here I lay, falling like a star in the dark of his wings.

I tell myself this delicate moment can last, that he'll say what I need to hear, the one thing liable to keep me. The dates vanish without words. I cuddle my whole body up against him, save for my ears, which lay listening, teased by his every breath.

A knock at the front door breaks our revelry. "Hello? Sheriff Blake?" The voice is high and light, clearly a young woman.

Both our ears pop up. Blake fumbles about on the bed, tangled in the sheets. Even with me in his life, he spends most of his nights dangling from the rafters. "Just a moment!"

I shake off a sudden tension. Usually, when folk come flying into a room unannounced, my guns practically jump into my paws. Maybe it's lessened with only the one? Composing myself, I swallow the last of the date flavor, now cloying from the shock of the interruption. I hop off the bed and into my shirt and trousers. A couple cinches and my belt and gunbelt. I tug my hat down my ears with a look to my lover. Lawbat's still doing a lopsided flutter into his vest when I'm fully decent. So I open the door and slip into the hallway.

At the front door, framed by the ember glow of evening, stands a collie. After an instant, I recognize her: the barkeep's daughter. Not used to seeing her outside the store room of the local saloon. She's a thin and fluffy thing, with deliberate motions covering a buzz of energy. She lifts floppy ears at me. "Oh! Mr. Shooter! I didn't think to see you here."

"Just had a little business with the good sheriff." I grin in a wheedling way and lean against a wall. Good thing I have a fine poker face. "What's brings your pretty self by?"

She yaps with surprise, silk tail taking a demure drop. "Two ferrets are having a terrible argument outside the saloon. Father said to get the law involved, on account of all the biting last time."

Blake emerges from the bedroom.

I nod his way. "Trouble in the ferret quarter."

Blake sits up, like nothing scandalous was occurring. "Another tinsel dispute?"

Her fluffy paws flutter like exotic moths. "It's something about an heirloom watch."

He straighten an inch or so taller. "I'll handle it."

"Nah, lawbat. Let me untangle the polecats."

"You sure?"

"Gotta earn mah keep as your fellow sheriff." Herded by the collie, I duck out the door and scamper down dusty streets to the bar.

↯ ↯ ↯

Outside the saloon, I pat the taller ferret on the back as he climbs aboard the stagecoach. "So glad we could settle this little quarrel."

"You're lucky I have business to see too, young hob!" He bends backward over my paw, snapping at the other party in the dispute. "Thievery is unbecoming habit in a ferret."

The smaller, scruffier ferret winces and minces. "But! But it wasn't yours—"

I hush the boy with a stern glance. This close to solving matters, I don't need more blabber and blubber. I murmur amiable assurances to the ferret in the bright-buttoned suit as I thread him into the stagecoach.

Paying me no heed, he brandishes a strip of paper. "Well, I have a receipt, so it's mine."

With a polite shove to the back of his exceptionally long waistcoat, I wrangle the polecat into the cab and shut the door. Best to get this trouble out of Blake's town presently. I hop to the front and slip the coach driver a fiver. "Get him to his train on time."

The plump prairie dog perks straight up with a chatter and a salute. "Yes, sir!" Scarcely waiting for me to get clear, he snaps the reins and stirs the ponies to a canter. In a matter of moments, the whole affair rattles off in a cloud of dust.

I watch him go with a smile. Double-stitched that tear in the fabric of society. Doubt even the lawbat couldn't have done it better. I turn to see the younger ferret slumped halfway to the ground with dejection.

The instant I touch the watch, whispers tease just at the edge of my hearing. Just like when I first examined it, I'm struck by an odd compulsion to tell the younger ferret to straighten his whiskers and brush his hat. The watch is about average, as echoes run. But even a quiet echo's enough to make something a treasured heirloom. The unearthly whisper between the ticks urge me toward the scruffy ferret. They silence only when I drop it in his paws.

The kit's sorrow is scattered in a burst of joy. He clutches the antique pocket watch to his chest. Words catch in his throat, at last tumbling out as a grateful chitter.

I tousle his ears. "Keep better track a' yer grandfather's favorite watch."

"How'd you know...?" He blinks, studying me. Even with perked-straight posture, he scarcely comes up to my chest.

"A bunny hears things." I toss an ear over my shoulder to make the point. "Now skedaddle." I tilt my head toward the nightly rabble and revelers gathering at the saloon. "Getting late out here."

He give a sweet little nod and scrambles off. Does my heart good to see him done right by. World sure wasn't doing right by me at that age.

Smiling, I watch the kit scamper off. Hardly any challenge in picking pockets when the plunder helps you steal it. I start on a strut back to the City Office. Blake makes this sheriffing business out to be troublesome, but he's of an overcomplicating bend. A rider comes trotting into town the way the carriage went, and for a moment, I worry it's the business ferret coming back. But then I recognize the ample ears and sad eyes of Blake's bloodhound deputy.

"Howdy, Six Shooter." Harding's droopy jowls sway as he dismounts. "Surprised to see you still in town."

"Not as surprised as me." Feeling personable, I slap him on the back. "Where ya been, deputy dog?"

He leads the pony by the halter. "Had to ride out to meet some 'yotes."

"Oh?" I walk abreast with him through the center of town. "What're they yapping about these days?"

He shrugs, like he expected me to know. "Giving back that tortoise."

I chuckle. "Tortoise?" And I thought my watch affair was petty; meanwhile, the deputy is herding turtles. "Must have been a dandy if they wanted it back."

"Surely was." He gives a little wag of pride. "That little turquoise one Blake had."

My ears fire straight up. "Does the lawbat know ya did this?" I round on the him.

The hound shies back. "Sure hope so." His tail ducks between his legs. "He's the one who had me do it."

I'm already bounding back down the streets and alleys. The blood-hound calls after me, but I pay him no mind. I've got a lawbat to straighten out.

↓ ∿ ↓

Dust stirs under my boots, lit red in the sunset. I bounce down the street and skid in front of the City Office. Hopping inside, I burst into the lawbat's office. "Ya gave it away!"

Quick feet steady his inkpot, which I'd rattled knocking the door open. He's pressed and dressed, showing no sign of our little encounter before. He raises his ears at me. "If you're referring to the tortoise arti-fact, yes. I gave it to the coyotes, its rightful owners. Harding assured me it would be a token of peace and respect between us." He sets his pen down. "Good evening to you too, Six."

"Ah never reckoned you'd just toss it at the first 'yote wanderin' by." I cross my arms. "Fool probably sold it for scrap. It'll be a yard a' telegraph line within the month."

"You can't be mad that I gave it to someone who'd appreciate it even more." He crosses his wings back at me. "And I sent the dear deputy to deliver it personally to the local chief."

My head tilts back with a groan. "That's almost as bad."

He smiles "We can always go on another adventure and get another one."

I'm struck with a sullen sulk. "No. You ruin 'em."

"I thought you might say that." He reaches into his vest pocket. "So I made you a peace offering too."

My gaze follows as he places a small whittled turtle in my paw. It's roughly the same shape as the one we "liberated," though of pine instead of copper. Anger flashes across my face, and for a moment I'm tempted to chuck it out the window. But then I look it over with a resigned air and place it carefully in my pocket. "Well, it's less trouble than the original."

A little smile spreads on his muzzle. "You get that stolen watch busi-ness sorted?"

"Surely did." I tug the front of my hat toward him, trying to ignore the little flicker of anger still lit in my chest. "Gave it to the rightful owner."

A moment passes. His ears rise. "How?"

"Hm?" I glance out the window as the color drains from the sky, like the world's wonder turning grey and cold. I don't look at Blake.

"How'd you figure out who to give it back to?" The lawbat plants his wings on his desk and leans forward. "Based on what evidence?"

"The weasels weren't lyin': that watch had an echo." I breathe, pinning and unpinning my borrowed badge. "It's sorted. So what's all the fuss about?"

His pretty eyes close in frustration. "That wouldn't stand up in court." The fading light glances off the badge, spilling across his face like 'yote warpaint.

I flash him a smirk, hoping this'll breeze on by. "Come on, lawbat. Nobody'd have gone to court if ya hadn't blabbed about it."

He straightens and crosses his wings in a lecturesome manner. "Six, I let you play sheriff for the day because I trusted you, and then you stole something right in front of me."

"Play nothin'!" Dropping my paws on the desk, I lean in at him. "You got any idea how many things ah didn't steal today?"

Blake's ears flick back, biting each word like a bitter fruit: "It reflects poorly on a sheriff to associate with thieves."

Pain jumps into my chest, at its heels a shameful burn in my ears. For a moment, I stammer. When I sort myself back together, I find his words have run a dark and steely edge through my voice. "You oughta reflect less on how you're reflectin'..." I drive a claw into the desk between us. "...and more on whether ya want this thief around!"

Mouth open, Blake freezes. Guess I wet the powder of whatever lawyerly argument he had loaded. His muzzle closes and starts working through every feeling he's got.

We stand quiet. Blood pounds through my ears. Boards creak under my boots as I shift weight, almost as loud as my jaw clenching, sealing in words I don't mean.

He glances down at the desk, then steps around it. The hot and cold of our chat leaves his tone tempered, but just as passioned. "I'm not ashamed of you, Six. I want you here. I-I..." A wing settles on my arm.

I tense, but don't shrug it off. Even I ain't that big a fool. Once I'm a few breaths older and wiser, my paw rises to cover his wing thumbs.

"Doc and Charlotte smoothed down the ruffled fur." He grips just a little. "You don't have to go."

The evening's events rattled me enough, it's a wonder my voice's not shaking now that I've cooled some. "'Fraid ah do, lawbat." I unclasp my hand from his, then the badge from my vest. All business-like, reach past him and set it on his desk.

"Six..."

"Hush now, lawbat." I unfix the pin I hold so dear, place it in his palm, and close his wing fingers over it it. "Take care a' this, will ya?"

Blake nods. His whole wing trembles like parchment spilled black with exotic ink.

I pull him in tight, holding him soft and gentle, trying not to see the hurt I'm leaving in his eyes.

He touches my face, like nobody else does, like I'm something breakable. "How am I supposed to figure us out if all you do is leave? When are we going to sort this out?"

I give him a quieting kiss, paws tracing over wings as I breeze toward the door. "One day, lawbat. One day."

Chapter 3

"Well, it's mine! Ah can steal mah own things!"

Sun's burning down another Arizona summer day. The thought of seeing the lawbat sends me skipping down the street—an unseemly means of locomotion for a gunslinger, perhaps, but sometimes I denying my bunny nature isn't worth the fuss. Besides, the townsfolk aren't exactly loitering in the desert heat. I bounce in the door of the City Office and into the little entertaining room.

Blake's eyes pop wide. He swings, claws around a rafter. A book falls from his wings to the plush settee. "Six!"

"Hey, sugarwings." I knock my hat off. Striding up, I bend to plant a kiss on his foxish muzzle. The moment hangs like my batty lover.

His wings spread, set aglow by sunlight. They wrap around me like gentle velvet. "Mmmm..."

Pulling back from the kiss, I stroke his upside-down ears with a little wink. "Knew you'd be missin' me."

He settles a soft touch settles on my shoulder, looking only a little sorrowful. "Like the fresh rain of spring, like the first peach of summer, like the cool of autumn."

In spite of the heat, a whole different kind of warmth kindles in my chest. I grin like a fool. Can't help swooning a little when the lawbat gets poetical.

A shock of wry crops up in his voice. "But none of those arrive in my town when I'd like." He crosses his wings over that shining badge. "So, what's the occasion?"

Touching a paw to my breasts, I mock offense. "Why, Sheriff Blake! Can't a bun just show up 'cause she's sweet on ya?"

"Can, but doesn't." His ears tilt back as his eyes study me. The ghost of our fight haunts the room. "But I am glad to see you safe."

I sigh, watching the dust stir off my long coat. "Safe, but none too pleased."

Hope raises his ears only an inch. "Grown weary of life on the road?"

"Weary of that lion slippin' through my fingers." My paws ball up into fists. "Was trackin' some a' Hayes' lackeys, some tiger and another cat in black. Lost the trail, but traced him back to a California ghost town."

He sighs, disappointed. "So you're going there next?"

"Me nothin'." I poke him in the chest, rocking him back and forth. "We've got a train to catch."

Still upside down, his eyebrows drop. "Do we now?"

"Sure as shootin'." I snag the tickets from my waistcoat pocket and wave them above his nose. "Ah found ya a spot of adventure to brighten up yer dreary lawfulness."

He hooks a wing finger on the beam, then swoops to stand. His eyes roll. "My gratitude is boundless." He makes no move to take the tickets.

I study him a moment. "Come on, lawbat. You're not still sour about me leavin', are ya?"

"I am."

"Ah'm sorry, Blake." A paw claps to my eyes and rolls back to flatten my ears. "Got a whole mess of desert to sift if ah'm gonna find that lion."

"That doesn't concern me." He stands his ground, fuzzy as a gooseberry, grim as a gander. "Your safety does."

My paws spread before him. "Ah'm made of stern stuff!" I pat my gunbelt. "Nobody's a faster draw or a surer shot."

"Or more full of hot air." He spreads his wings.

I pinch the bridge of my muzzle. "Jordan, if ya got a better idea, ah'm all ears." I pop them up to show I mean it.

He props his wings one his hips. "You could stay in town."

A reply sharpens on my tongue, but a whisper of restraint holds my fire. Got few enough friends in the world without rubbing my sweetheart the wrong way. Besides, I hate seeing him distressed. "Let's say ah do. How's a bun keep busy?"

His thin buffets up on the surprise of my being reasonable. He sweeps wing fingers to the window. "You could take up a profession."

I flip my hat back on and give him a pained look. "We tried that, remember?"

"You don't have to work with me." With lawyerly regard, he straightens his little vest. "Plenty of other options in White Rock. Good, honest work."

"Keen as ah am on honest work…" I shrug.

"Please, Six?" He bites his lower lip. "I can hardly get through the day without you here."

A tangle of feelings wiggle my nose. I should be mad he wants to pin me down, but I'm caught by his earnest gold-flecked eyes. All the gold in the world couldn't keep me from him, but one silver gun can. I want to tell him, but I stumble over words unspoken. In the end, all I can offer him is a smile of surrender.

He cracks a little smirk. "And scarcely make it through one with you."

I laugh. The tension breaks and crumbles. I slap him on the shoulder. "Can that sass and pack yer plunder." I kick his coat rack, catch the white hat that tumbles from it, and toss it to his chest. "We're lightin' a shuck for California."

With a resigned look, he tugs it on over his ears and rests his wings on his gunbelt. "California?" He shakes his head at me. "You get a sleeper car, at least?"

⩗ ⩑ ⩗

We hares have always seen a bunny in the moon, stirring a pot over a fire. The particulars on just what's getting stirred change, of course, with who you ask. Medicine or magic, dreams or disasters, the cold sea tides or the heat of a bunny's monthly. I've heard tell, in the Orient, the Bun in the Moon makes rice taffy. Me, I'm keen on the witch's brew version, since I just seem to stir up trouble.

Just another bunny under the moonlight, I lay in the narrow bed and feel the train clatter and shake under me. That endless rumble can wear on the mind of those not used to it. I don't travel much by rail, so it proves mighty distracting: don't know why folk bother calling these sleeper cars. Lucky for me, I've got a certain lawbat between my legs for distraction. Behind the cover of the little bed curtain, we see about a little jostling of our own. That cute little flying fox face dives between my thighs and sets to licking. His tongue traces my slit and laps deeper and deeper into me. I press buck teeth to my lower lip as my paws trail under my shirt to play with my nipples. Minutes and miles trundle past as I lay back smiling.

Last I checked, we had the car to ourselves, but I bite back my moans all the same. Wouldn't do to perk up curious ears, not when I'm getting lost in Blake finding all my most sensitive spots. His nose is buried in my mound now and he's licking up my juices with naked enjoyment. His trousers are undone and one wing is brushing the curtain with each stroke as he rubs that pretty pink length of his. A bead of excitement shines at the blunt tip. I squirm at the hard evidence of just how much the sheriff takes to me.

With a bump along the tracks, my clit presses hard on his tongue, casting me over the edge. I lift my tail off the bed and a whimper from my lungs as his tongue twirls me through a whirlwind of shivering tension and honeyed ease.

As I come down from the heights, I'm struck with a powerful need to have him inside me. I tug at his ears, all gentle and urgent. Smiling, he crawls up my body. It's a bit cramped, but we get matters sorted in short order. He's too wound up and I'm too unwound for even the barest scrap of modesty. My paw closes around his girth and guides it just where it belongs. I stroke the supple skin up and down, urging him on. With a press of his hips, he sinks in. My toes curl against the sheets as he fills me. The beat of his heart throbs against my tender, clutching passage. I close my eyes and feel him rock in and out of me, stirring up slick pleasure around that lovely length.

We move together, the sounds of our passion hidden by the clatter of the train. The good sheriff thrusts all frantic as his wings grip my hips. Must've been pent up since my last visit. I find his eagerness right agreeable, my body rising to meet his, helping him hit all manner of fine places within me. His ragged breaths warm my nose and caress my throat fluff. I meet his gaze with all my tenderness and nearly all my trust to whisper: "Oh Jordan…"

With a squeak and a shudder, he goes off. A swell of heat spreads from the tip of his cock through my innermost places. A different kind of warm kindles in my heart as he slumps onto me, spent and sticky. I slip my arms around his shoulders and stroke his hair and ears. Wary as I am of the world, he makes me want to close my eyes and trust in the warmth of his embrace, even as the juices running down to my tail take on a slight chill.

As his breaths level out, those wings fold around me like living velvet. My pleasure-addled brain reckons I ought to stay within reach of those wings all the time. Can't go anywhere without thinking about the fool, so he's got me surrounded anyway.

I nuzzle in close and enjoy the soft orange fluff of his throat, lit silver in the moonlight. He calls me pretty. It's nice to have a fella who calls me pretty. And Blake ought to know: spends every day being too pretty for his own good.

There's road left to put my boots on before I could think about settling down with him, most of it chasing the lion who stole my father's other gun. I admit I was surprised to find the good sheriff willing to come with me on this little excursion.

ᙖ ᠕ ᙖ

Right on schedule, my train stops in the middle of nowhere.

I step out the door, dust stirring in a curl under by boots. Nice when a bun can just bribe her way into getting a train to stop, rather than pulling the emergency cord. Out of respect for my dear Sheriff Blake, I took to calling it a "tip" so as not to offend his delicate sensibilities.

The lawbat hops off beside me, wings spread to break the fall. His dainty travel case dangles from slender wing-fingers. "Just looking for information, right? You're not going to cause trouble?"

My eyes meet Blake's and glimpse the home our hearts've been building. I'd better be careful or he'll manage to keep hold of me for good. I've got a heap of bad to do before then. "When've ah ever caused you trouble?"

The locomotive belches black smoke above and spits steam to either side. With a rolling rumble, it thunders to motion and leaves us standing in the middle of the sun-baked desert.

Blake watches the train chug and rattle into the distance. His fancy little vest gleams against the red dust. It's jet black with a whole patch of embroidered strawberry vines flourishing across the front. Even the buttons blossom with little painted white-and-yellow strawberry flowers.

I shoulder my rucksack and follow the old branch line south. Spy the old fort a couple miles down, then peek back for another glimpse of that dandy garment, unable to keep from smiling. "Speaks to my fondness that ah'm willin' to be seen with such a duded-up lawbat."

"This is perfectly reasonable attire for a shopping holiday." He brushes the dust from it. "You failed to mention we'd be disembarking in the middle of desolate nowhere." He pads up beside me and straightens fully, though not enough to pass my chin. "Besides, my family says these Polish-style vests are quite the craze."

My eyes roll at his hoity-toity notions. "We're over the border, lawbat. This is California: land a' gold, grit, and gunsmoke. Folk round here don't give a whit about fruity fashion."

"I'll grant you it's not suitable for when I'm on duty." He pats his travel bag with a fond wing. "It's far less overstated than my grapevine one, however. Or even the peach tree one."

I refrain from informing him what I think the peach one looks like.

We hike down the dusty rails as the ghost town comes into view. A collection of shacks huddles around a pale adobe fort. Several spots on it bear char marks, where someone learned you can't burn down an earthen wall.

He gives it a sidelong look. "You're sure this place is above board?"

I shrug. "Might bilk a fool now and then, but from what ah've heard, when it comes to trading echoes, there's no finer establishment."

"I'll need you to nail down some of these specifics for me." He straightens his gunbelt, looking to the silver gun on mine. "What echoes can and can't do."

Muzzle tilted down, I cast a coy glance his way. "Why've you gotta make everything about rules?"

His wings cross over that fine little vest. "Rules are how we make sense of the world."

"Fine, fine." I tug my hat down against the hot wind. "Rule one: near as ah can figure, only trinkets with some amount of the ore can echo." I pat my father's gun, still a trifle tender about a certain lion pilfering the second one. Ought to let him keep a few of the bullets when I get it back.

"I see." Blake dances as his bare toe touches the sun-hot train rail.

I struggle not to smile. "Rule two: gotta be handled by somebody a while before they kick the bucket."

The lawbat nods, all studious. How his professors put up with him at that highfalutin law college, I'll never know.

"Rule three: some folk are better than others at hearin' echoes." I raise my ears to the hot wind, but hear nothing save the scour of sand and the whisper of weeds. "Some can't do it worth a lick, such as you."

He rolled his eyes, looking more like gold dust than coffee grounds in this light. "Then why bother bringing me?"

"In case ah get walloped by an echo and keel over. Folk get shady this far out in the desert." I put on a dignified look for him. "A lawman's pistol at their backs oughta head off any riflin' through mah pockets."

"Delightful." The lawbat crosses his wings. "Never let it be said you don't take me nice places."

I lean within nibbling distance of his ear. "Seem to recall takin' you all kinds of nice places in the sleeper car last night."

That flusters him some.

My boots crunch along the dusty ground. "Must admit ah'm pleased you don't think I'm buying into old legends."

"The evidence falls on the side of echoes being more than superstition, foremost among which is your not being dead." He examines the claw of a wing finger. "That said, I would take it as a kindness if you took fewer risks."

I shrug. "World's a dangerous place."

His look sharpens to a glare. "Especially around you."

"Exactly." I grin. "'Sides, ah got lov—" My hot ears drop against the brim of my hat. "—luck on mah side and the law by it. That counts for something."

He flutters his wings on the hot breeze. "You'll have an easier time convincing me of echoes from the afterlife than luck."

We walk a distance further. I can see a figure slinking along the high adobe walls. Some manner of cat. A long rifle glints in his paw. I can tell by the tilt of his ears that he's got an eye for us.

Unaware, Blake clears his throat. "The family back east has been after me to visit. If you're game for another train ride after this, I'd welcome your company, to say nothing of your support."

I grimace. "'Fraid ah'd scandalize the delicate darlings."

He snickered a little laugh of agreement. "Maybe we should start with your relations."

"Ah'd scandalize them worse."

We near the massive wooden gate. A sun-bleached sign arches above it: Fort Calico.

The heavy door swings open.

A full set of wolverine teeth come out to greet us. "You here to cause trouble?"

"No, ma'am." Blake straightens to show off his badge.

A moment blows by on the dusty breeze.

My thumb traces the brim of my hat. "You lettin' us in?"

Greed and fear wrestle on her face. With a shallow snarl, she waddles back from the door. She's squat, like a cast-iron stove, and a slight curl to her lips hints at temper simmering behind those brown eyes. "What'd ya want?"

"Some particulars." My arms cross over my breasts. "Maybe lookin' to make purchases. Ah've heard talk you sell echoes."

She studies us more, like anybody could make sense of me traveling with a fancy little thing like Blake. Her heavy fists plant on stout hips.

I scoff, though I make sure I'm clear of those clawed hands first. "You always so friendly to customers?"

"C'mon." The wolverine stumps back toward the buildings.

The bat and I trade looks. He sweeps a wing out like a gentleman, his grin saying he's happy to have me deal with the charming old wolverine.

Pass by an number of battered buildings on our way. Most look to have been here since the construction of the fort. All look in need of repair. We arrive at what used to be the general store. The cat opens the front door for us. A woozy feeling rushes over me, followed by whispers on the edge of hearing, whispers not of the living world. One more step and the world's awash in whispers—it's sweeping me away until strong wing fingers close around my elbow. I blink and grit my teeth, dropping my ears and fix a serious on my muzzle.

We amble inside the shop. Shelves offer a whole mess of items: sacks of grain, boxes of bullets, tins of salt and pepper. Everything from clothes to kettles hang from the rafters, with barrels of sugar, vinegar, flour, and molasses standing guard below.

The trader stomps behind the till. She sweeps a thick paw at the trays of glimmering baubles lining the counter. Silver, mostly, with the odd rock tossed in.

"That's some ace-high jewelry." I tilt my ears back and smile all charming. "Where ya keepin' the echoes?"

She leans forward on the counter. "Maybe you're not listening close enough."

"Bosh. These wouldn't echo a cuss in a cave." I tilt a finger down at the gewgaws. "That much mirror ore shoulda knocked me flat on mah tail." My fingertip slides the tray to one side, all slow and serious. "Ah'm lookin' for silver that won't tarnish, guns that aim yer hands."

Those wolverine teeth show up again, this time in a smile, which is only a touch less alarming. She turns her head to shout upstairs. "Striker! Get your tail down here. And bring the goods."

A bobcat pads down the stairs with a grin and two bandoleers. By the slink of his step, I'd venture he's the one who watched us from the wall. In his paws, he's got a strongbox and a bottle of wine. He fishes four glasses from behind the counter and lines them up on the counter. With a few deft motions, he slices the sealing wax with a claw, cranks a corkscrew in, and tugs the cork free with a deep plunk. In his spotted paw, the red wine flows in easy arcs into each glass. Pours a little extra into the last one, but he sees to that glass himself.

Our host produces a box of cigars, gnaws the end off one, and sets the other end in her muzzle.

With a snap of clawed fingers, the cat flicks a match from nowhere and lights her cigar.

I snicker. "That how you got your name?"

"One of the reasons, amigo." Another snap flares a match against his paw pads and straight at me. The sputtering flame whizzes through my whiskers in a streak of brimstone.

I try to make my freezing from surprise look like grit. "Well, mah name's Six Shooter." I let one paw drop to my father's gun. "If ya need a demonstration a' why, just say."

Sheriff Blake fires a warning look at me.

I sit on a barrel of sugar, smiling just as sweet. Few things in life leave as bitter a taste as my lawbat being right. No sense letting that fool stir me up.

"Oooh, fiery." The feline rumbles a flirtatious purr my way and prowls forward on the counter. "I like men who are a little dangerous."

My ears drop in a furious blush. He couldn't possibly know I'm a woman. No. This furball's toying with me. Either he's trying to rile me, or he's actually taken a shine. I find my mouth stammering, so I clamp it shut and ignore the heat under my cheek ruffs. Damn sly bobcat, making a fool out of me.

"Striker, don't burn my store down." Cigar in her teeth, the trader throws a damp rag onto the match smoldering on her floor, which dies with a hiss. "And don't make a mash on the customers." After a few puffs, she waves the cigar at us. "You mind if I smoke?"

"Why would we?" Surly, I hook my thumbs in my gunbelt. "Blowin' smoke's about all you've done since we got here."

A big growl of a laugh cuts through the room. "I can't go sellin' my best wares to any fool walking in the door. Most folks want good-luck charms and worry stones. They want their fill of a story and half a mystery for their money."

I lean forward on the barrel and keep my ears down to hide the blush. "Not the pony ah'm fixin' to buy."

"No, I suppose not." Her heavy paw closes around the flimsy glass.

The fruit bat, looking wholly too amused, swirls his wineglass with a cordial grin. "You'll have to excuse my companion. He gets a little carried away now and again." He takes a seat on the barrel next to mine and sweeps a wing to his heart. "I'm Sheriff Jordan Blake, from White Rock. And you are...?"

"Minerva." The wolverine leans forward on the counter and lifts her own glass at the walls. "This trading fort's from the silver rush and I'm from ever since then." She nods to Striker.

The bobcat creaks open the box he brought.

Lid's only open a hair when I catch a rush of strange whispers. My ears go up, though that doesn't help a bit. Echoes.

Sunlight gleams inside the gold-lined cases. Voices trail in and out, just on the edge of hearing. Mournful, joyful, spiteful: none of them meaning to talk to me, but talking nonetheless. I struggle to quiet down my thoughts, to grab hold of even one of those voices, but it's like grasping at the mist. Whole world fades from me, but I'm stretching out with my mind, straining after words I almost hear...

Striker closes the box.

I look around. Lost a moment or two, judging by the concern the Sheriff's giving me. I scoot back from the very edge of the sugar barrel and play like I didn't just get dragged to distraction by the yammering of the dead. "Boss boxes ya got."

Minerva puffs on her cigar. "Pure gold blocks the echoes."

"And here I mistook your actions for unalloyed greed." Blake pats my shoulder, wine glass in his other wing.

The bobcat chuckles and laps drops of wine from his whiskers. His gaze hints at several parts of me he might like a lick at, which may or may not exist.

"Where'd ya get all that, anyhow?" I lift my chin at the box on the countertop.

"Here and there. Some folks dumped their echoes when the current trouble started." She drums her claws on the lid of the box. "As for the pieces at the counter, the 'yotes trade me those silver and turquoise pieces. I ship the greater portion back east, since almost none of 'em echo. Or ever could."

I cross my arms over my breasts. "How do you sort the silver from the mirror ore?"

She scratches her wide gut. "Trade secret."

"Ah reckon the real thing sells better." My ears rise. "Why don't they make tons of the stuff?"

"It's tied to the spirits of the dead. Most tribes have an aversion to the dead." Her teeth shred more cigar smoke to thin, gray ribbons. "Even among the 'yotes, you've gotta be part of their 'ghost society' to deal in echoes."

The fruit bat cocks his head and fires off a skeptical glance. "Ghost society?"

"It is a social club, good sheriff..." Striker purrs through his Rs from where he leans on the counter. His caramel-brown eyes shift to my companion as the cat toys with a whisker. "...where coyotes ask the dead for secrets."

A snag of jealousy catches in my chest. I fix a stern look on my muzzle and turn to the wolverine. "Just how's that work?" My paw traces the handle of my father's revolver. I've only talked to my father through echoes the one time and I'd rather not repeat the steps that led up to that.

"If you find out, come tell me." The stocky mustelid leaned back, her smoke drifting to the rafters. "I'll make you the richest bunny this side of the Mississippi."

I ponder, for a moment, just how rich that would be. More than once, Blake's asked just what I'd do with a pile of money. Maybe put out a reward for the return of my missing firearm. "Ah'm lookin' for a gun like this one." Easy and slow, so as to avoid misunderstandings, I draw the gun and hold it by the barrel. "Don't suppose you've seen anything like that?" I tug the silver revolved from its holster, then grab it by the barrel and show it to her.

Beady wolverine eyes squint at it. Her wide snout grumbles closer. She grits her teeth at the gun for a second. "Hmf! Wish we got more pieces that strong. A lion came in with one of those, sure. Just like it, in fact. Eager to sell it."

I bounce upright with hope. "So ya bought it from him?"

"Of course not." The badger crosses her thick arms. "The fool clearly stole it. And his asking price was terrible. Said something about trading an entire silver mine for it. Too much trouble."

"Too much trouble!" I yank my ears in fury. "Ah could've just bought the thing back!" I arch back under the weight of how unfair this all is.

The lawbat pats me with a wing. "Let's be honest: you'd have just stolen it."

It round on him. "Well, it's mine! Ah can steal mah own things!"

The shopkeepers watch me scowl at him, in smug silence.

Enjoying my discomfort, Blake takes another sip of the wine. His talented little tongue rolls over his pearly whites, collecting every trace of the sip. "This is quite good wine."

The trader nods. "If you're interested, I've got a selection of fruit bat liqueurs."

A snap of mischief breaks me from my despair. I keep my face stone serious. "Bats do make the finest lickers."

The lawbat chokes on his second sip.

Hiding my smile behind the wine glass, I get down to brass tacks. "Why all this fuss? Can't be good for business."

"We're a tight little bunch, echo enthusiasts. Wary of newcomers at the best of times. Then I had three of my contacts turn up dead in the last month." She tapped a little ash toward Striker. "Times being what they are, I'd already taken on additional security."

Blake's ears go up. "Dead?"

"Only heard about it second-hand, but my regulars have scattered to the winds." Her gaze drifted out the door to the barred front gate. Just when or who had barred it, I wasn't sure. "Figure I'd hunker down till this trouble blows by. Pity. Have a fair inventory built up."

"I suppose you'd have to be careful." Blake finishes his wine and settles his wings. "Too much mirror ore seems to just leave everyone shambling around."

"Echoes are powerful." Smoke curls up through her grinning fangs. "Some veins run under ghost towns, having driven every soul screaming mad."

Holstering, I scoff at her theatrics. "Speakin' of ghost towns, how do ya stay in business?" My eyes dance over the wares and windows. "Not exactly bustling around here."

"Oh, I manage." The wolverine hauls another drag on her cigar. "Local elk tribes come down from their high desert plazas to stock up. You'd be surprised how happy they are to get their hooves on modern salt lick and antler ornaments. Want nothing to do with echoes, of course: ghost fear. Good weavers, though." She hooks a thumb claw at a row of fine cotton sheets, which are about the first thing I'd buy without a worry in this place.

I eye the door.

Blake pats my knee. "Now, Six: our train home won't pass by for another few hours. It'd be rude not to peruse their wares."

A ferocious grin rises to our host's muzzle. "I can see you're a gentleman of taste, Mister Blake." She draws a wooden case from under the counter. "Perhaps I could interest you in this." Clawed hands draw a timepiece on a fob chain from the padded inside of the box. "A skeleton watch, it's called. They're the height of fashion in Europe, only now landing on the Atlantic shore."

Through the glass face of the thing, I see every moving part. The inside of each gear has been whittled away to let you see clear through to the back of the case. A diverting novelty, to be sure, but who'd need a thing like that?

"Fascinating." He extends a polite wing. "May I see?"

"Of course." She hands it over with excessive care, hoping to inflate its value further.

I groan. Now the old lady won't be satisfied until she's shown us every gimcrack and knickknack in the place.

Blake brings the ticking trinket in for a closer look. A tangle of clockwork clicks and twirls in perfect order. Stands to reason the lawbat would like it.

"Best not be an echo in the thing." I narrow my gaze on the watch, then at its seller. "All ah need is some departed deer whispering salad recipes whenever ah'm around you."

Her paw waves in a gesture that says not to worry, which I find worrying.

"I'll take it." He sweeps a wing forward, all elegance and refinement. "Six, pay the woman."

My attention flashes to Blake. "Use yer own money!"

He straightens his vest and lifts his chin over my objections. "Considering how many of my possessions go missing, I believe I am."

I grumble as I fish the bills from my wallet. Gonna need some payback later from the lawbat for being right all over the place. Maybe back in the sleeper car, where I can get him right where I want him.

This trio of fools wastes another hour of my time. The wolverine waddles and puffs through the shelves. The bobcat smarms my way and eyes my tail to within one glance of getting a punch to the face. Besides the watch, Blake picks himself out a broach and some extra-warty squashes. At least, I reckon the broach is for him—sheriff's not gonna pin anything like that on me.

Never thought I'd be so glad to leave a place I dragged Blake to. Hauling his purchases, we cut back down the main street of the ghost town.

Striker walked us out with a rogue's grin. "Goodbye, handsome."

Poking his whiskered face through the gap between the gates, he tips a battered leather hat my way. "Come back soon so we can compare guns." With a wink, he shuts the gate before I can reply. I hear a heavy wooden beam bar it.

I grumble and turn away, but hold my tongue until we're out of earshot. Over my shoulder, I sling a bag with the greater share of the squashes. My boots crunch down the trail back to the main rail line. "Ah can't believe that cat. The nerve!"

The bat chuckles into a wing. "Yes, imagine the scandal if an outlaw acted like that in the town where you're sheriff. People would talk."

Can't find an answer to that, so I stomp on down the road.

The bat dips his muzzle and flashes those gold-flecked eyes my way. "You did come here for information."

I sulk onward.

A long moment and several hundred feet of rail pass.

Blake grins like a fool, examining his shiny new watch. "Quite a woman, that Minerva."

Rolling a cigarette with one paw, I croak a laugh. "An old battle-axe, ya mean."

He traces a wing thumb down my arm. "Perhaps I have an affection for formidable women."

"Perhaps you'd best not count us as peas in a pod if ya aim to see any affection from me." I cast him a glance from the corner of my eye. "She's built like an ironclad warship and billows smoke like a coal-fired engine."

"Then I beg your pardon, madam." He sweeps his hat off in a smooth batty bow. "An ironclad doesn't do justice to your ceaseless and unjustified belligerence."

I pause in the middle of licking the rolled paper sealed. "Is that sass ah hear from mah upstandin' lawbat?"

"Entirely possible." His smile turns my way. "Afraid I've fallen in with an uncouth crowd of late."

As I set the squash bag by the rail junction, my ears rise to the distant chug of a locomotive nearing from the west.

In the fading evening, Blake fishes our tickets from his embroidered vest pocket as he checks his fine new pocket watch. "Right on time."

I stand on the rails, facing down the train. My duster blows in the breezes, all aglow as I light a cigarette. I may be a trifle stubborn, but I reckon it'll take a mite of stubbornness to get my father's other gun back. If that makes me a little like that that old wolverine, then so be it.

Chapter 4

"Even a gunslinger needs a little reassurin'."

I walk my patrol, rather than flying, just to enjoy the night. The town as dark as it is quiet, unusual for a full moon. Only the distant blotch of a thunderhead foreboded any disruption of the peaceful night. As I take a deep breath of cool night air, I take pride in the fact I have something to do with bringing peace to this area.

With the streets awash in moonbeams, I scarcely need to echolocate. My occasional tongue-click keeps me from blundering into a tie-post. It does nothing to warn me about the ne'er-do-well watching me from the alley.

Her voice sweeps in a dusty drawl as I pass by: "Well, if it isn't mah pretty little lawbat."

My heart races. I turn to see a hare gunslinger leaning against a building. The cool glow of moonlight paints the rest of the world in silver, but a smoldering cigarette casts her in gold. Before I realize it, my feet carry me toward her. "Yours?"

She flicks her cigarette away and brushes a claw down the front of my vest. "Can't a bun lay claim?"

I adjust the brim of my hat, taking on a lawyerly tone. "It's my understanding of homesteading that a claimant has to stick around if they expect to get anything."

"And make improvements. Ah try my best there, but the going's tough." Mischief flashes in her eyes. "Plot's kinda small and outta the way, but ah peek in now and then."

I roll my eyes, but edge closer. I lift her chin, looking into her eyes. She might object, but I think she's lovely. In the dark of the alley, I steal a soft kiss.

She hooks a trigger finger into my vest and drags me into a much more scandalous kiss.

Blushing to the ears, I cast a paranoid glance to the street, only to find it empty. My wings close around her.

Our affections are interrupted by a crackle of thunder overhead.

She looks up, lifting her ears to the half-black sky. "Storm's rolling in."

I glance up in time to see another cascade of light tumble through the clouds. "Might be best if we got inside before we're caught in a deluge."

We share a smile and head back toward my office. I fumble my keys at the door as her paws meander to my backside. Her hat gets knocked off as we kiss in the hallway; it flutters to the floor with a woolen whisper.

If Six was bold in the moonlight, she's shameless in the dark. No sooner have I set the latch than she has me pressed against the wall. Her leg rises with my temperature as she nuzzles the fur of my neck.

I squirm at our lewd pose, feeling myself pulse to hardness. This bunny always manages to drive me wild in one way or another. Breath short, I stroke my fingertips down her tender ears, drawing a supple gasp from my rugged outlaw. I chuckle. "I missed you terribly."

"Aww, listen to you making a mash." She nuzzles me, her breath smoke, her tone silk. "Ah missed you too, sugarwings." With that, she slips an arm behind my back and knees and carries me down the hall to my room. We laugh together as she deposits me on the bed, then pauses to take off her gunbelt. She sets it on the nightstand, within a moment's reach, then climbs into bed with me.

I struggle out of my own gunbelt and drape it over the bedpost. In the dark, I hear the matched thunks of her boots dropping off the side of the bed. I draw up against her. With my thief beside me, I've never felt so safe.

Her touch runs down my wing like rain.

Those muscled arms roll me over as she climbs atop me. She leans in with a salacious smile. Her lips meet mine with warm desire.

My wing-fingers slip under her vest to weave through the fur of her back, then slip forward to undo the buttons. In no time, she's helping me out of my clothes too, then helping herself to all the pleasure my length has to offer. She rides hard as storm winds sweep down off the mountain. The bedstead rattles in reply to the shingles until we both tense, shudder, and collapse into drowsy satisfaction.

With her breath slowing in my ear, I glide into a blithe sleep.

↓ ≈ ↓

Morning comes in the blink of an eye.

I wake to watch Six dress. She notices me. Though smiling, the bunny bites her lip. Her boot twitches against the floorboards. "Ya always get my heart all balled up."

I prop myself up on a wing. "It's fair to say you do a number on my heart too."

"Ah know you're not the kind to tell a girl things you don't mean just to take her for a tumble." She winces. "But would it kill ya to lead a bun on?"

My blood runs colder than Skull Creek. "What do you mean?"

"Ah mean ah'd like to hear you say—" She chokes on rising emotion. "—that ya love me."

Deep down, I want to. But every time she leaves, there's fair odds she'll wind up dead in some random patch of desert and I'd never hear about it. She'd just vanish in the wind. "Six, I..."

With shocked anger, she gets to her feet. Booted footfalls clunk heavy on the floor as she tries to walk through a muddle of emotions. "Ah want to know somebody in this big lonely desert wants me around all the time." Her paw traces up her arm, strong fingers gripping scuffed sleeve fabric.

"I— You really are dear to me, Six." I reach out to her.

"Then say so." She draws back, temper flaring under the surface of her tone. "Even a gunslinger needs a little reassurin'."

"You need reassurance? I take you back every time you run off to risk your life for no good reason." I take a little breath to cool my anger. "What assurance do I have you won't just take my words and leave?"

A look, stubborn as iron, clamps over her muzzle. "It's mah business where ah go. Yer just gonna have to live with that."

I sit up straight, the fur on my neck prickled. "If you really believe that, you're as selfish as you are contrary. Your modus operandi thus far has been to only show up when you need something from me."

"You little lawyering son of a bitch! Don't try and turn this around on me." She swept a sheaf of paper from my nightstand. "Stop being a coward and say it!"

As paperwork fluttered down around me, I lower my muzzle and my tone. "I won't be railroaded into saying something I'm not fully certain of."

"Ah don't need you to be certain. Heck, I don't even need ya to mean it." She leans in, arms crossed as she scowls. "Whatever you're feelin', call it love. Ah dare you."

"And when you get yourself killed and I never find out? What then?"

"Get killed? You could catch a bullet tomorrow." The slim bunny shrugs. "Not all folk are as tolerant of a lawbat bossin' 'em around."

"I—" I clear my throat. "I hadn't thought of that."

"Glory be!" Her ears and arms raise in false exaltation. "A thing Sheriff Blake hasn't thought of."

I bite back a bitter retort. "So stick around. Watch my back."

She hesitates. The flick of her gaze away from me says she's either thinking it over or has done so already.

"Hayes drifted out of town after you blew up his mine." I sweep a wing toward the edge of town. "You're as safe here as anywhere."

Having talked each other to silence, we stew in it. She stares at my now-clear nightstand for a spell, then huffs down to seat herself on it. Our eyes meet, finding the words we can't. Minutes pass by as we sit speechless, alternating between close study of each other and looking away.

A gust of wind rattles my office, shaking us from our doldrums. Six stands and snatches her hat from the hallway floor.

I get to my feet, not knowing what I plan to do next. Stop her? This conversation established nothing if not my lack of ability on that front. And possibly hers.

She slips her ears through and tugs the hat in place. Her smile is slight, but directed at me. "Ah might be back sooner than later, ah guess."

I cross my wings and give my muzzle a slow shake. "I might be ready to say it then, I guess."

Six takes a halting step toward the door, then pulls a wingover back

to me. Her lips grace mine: lightly, softly. Then she's out the door and down the hall.

I watch as she opens the front door to a sky of clouds blushing at their false promise of rain.

She casts a little look back at me, this time with wry amusement. "Suppose it's good you have a backbone, Jordan."

I lean against the hallway wall. "You need a man who has one."

Her smile broadens a fraction, then she's out the door and out of my life for the time being. The door closes and she walks past the window of my sitting room. Above, the clouds roll on, not having spilled a drop.

Chapter 5

"Bubbles tickle mah nose."

My thief breezes into the office.

Silver pistol at her hip, blue steel at the other, the hare stands before my desk. A long coat sways in the hot breeze, dust trailing off like a vapor. That smoky muzzle gleams a smile under stormy eyes.

A quick paw locks the door. The bunny's boots ring on the floorboards. "Howdy, lawbat."

"Six…" A pen drops from my hind paw, staining the cuff of my trousers and making a Dalmatian of the document. I jump up, but not in time to save them. "Aw, heck!"

"That's a fine way to greet a lady." A touch out of breath, she tilts my muzzle up into a kiss. The ghost of a cigarette haunts her lips.

Warmth floods my wings. The ink-stained pants and the intervening time since our last kiss vanish from my concern, leaving only the bunny standing over me. The kiss ends in a little rub of noses. "So you're a lady now?"

"Much as ah've ever been." Her muzzle aligns on mine like a compass needle. I wish that compass didn't lead her so far afield between kisses.

"Who're you running from now?"

"Nobody with fair odds a' catchin' me."

"Fair odds and you don't run together." My wings trace around her hips, finding that fluff of a tail.

Her caress falls on my wings like Arizona rain. "Never hear you complain when they're in your favor."

We kiss again. Sunlight spills in around us, discernible even when I close my eyes, just like the bunny in my wings. Our muzzles slide along each other until our foreheads touch. The window's dusty and the door's locked; in this rare moment I'm alone with her.

"You could always stay." Whispering, I smile, a trifle unsteady.

"You could always go." Her paw grazes my badge.

Not wanting to dwell on impossibilities, I rise into another kiss, letting my tongue trail along her lips.

She giggles, backing off just a little. "Ease off there, sugarwings. Yer kissin' is a mite distractin'."

"Reckoned that's the point." I kiss the corner of her smile.

"You can distract me in a moment's time. Right now I got a little something for you." Her long coat slips down those elegant arms, showing the delicate shades of her fur. She withdraws something from a pocket, then drops the coat to the floor in a heap. A parcel sits in her grasp, brown paper blending with the tan of desert hare pelt.

My ears flatten. "Something you stole?"

"Bought—" She tilts the paper-wrapped object. "I know you're all particular."

"Bought with stolen funds."

Her claws scritch under my chin, her voice losing its edge and most of its smoke. Her ears go down. "Ya want what I got or not?"

Helpless against her bunny charms, my wing thumbs trace the curve of her back.

She kisses me down into my chair, handing me the gift.

Touching it strikes my wings like electricity. "It's cold!"

"That it is, lawbat."

I laugh, holding it gingerly. Seems today comes full of surprises. "You come across an icebox out in the desert?"

"You don't expect a bunny to go tellin' you all her secrets, do ya?"

I slip the parcel paper off it, finding it to be a bottle marked with exotic glyphs and symbols.

"Some manner a' Oriental sarsaparilla. Seein' as you're so keen on fruit."

I turn the jade glass bottle over and try to twist off the cap. "Sarsaparilla's not a— Wait, how'd you come to know what it says?"

Pushing aside the papers, she sits on my desk. "Got it from an otter chemist in California."

"And you take his word on that?" I struggle at opening it with my wings, since reaching up with a hind paw would be uncouth.

"Gave him cause to tell me the truth." Her powerful legs cross before me. "Try it. I don't reckon it's even liquor. Least I think that's what he said. Talked a mite funny."

"You —huuh!— inspire nothing but confidence, madam." I wrestle with the cap.

She snatches the bottle from my wings and raps it hard against the edge of my desk. The cap pops off, leaving little gouges in the wood. Her deft paws spin it back to eye level, not spilling a drop.

I nod. "Much obliged."

"Ah hate to see a lawbat in peril." She sweeps that hat off her ears. They sway, translucent in the midday sun, causing my heart to flutter like a bat's first flight. Smiling, she places the bottle at my lips.

I open my mouth with care. Cold floods my tongue, then sweetness. Effervesce prickles through my mouth. I lick my lips, then grin. "It's good."

She leans in closer, amused no doubt at my halfwitted reaction. An affectionate paw brushes my cheek. My wing thumbs curl around the bottle but she doesn't let go.

"Try some."

Her head shakes. "Bubbles tickle mah nose." Her pink nose twitches.

I raise my ears and eyebrows. We let time hang a moment.

She relents, releasing her grasp.

I lift the bottle to her lips. The chill of glass stands in sharp contrast with the heat in her fur. The moment can't last, I know; the bottle will empty and she will be gone. Yet, as she takes a tentative swallow, those paws gentle on my wings, none of that matters.

A bead of sarsaparilla runs down my wing thumb, cold as well water. The hare raises my fingers to her lips, licking them clean. "Not bad." She smiles.

My wings flush with heat. I wish I could blame the sun, or something in the drink, but I know the reason is slipping off my desk right now, straddling my lap.

"Ah keep showin' up like this, folk'll wonder if you're knockin' boots with a tall bunny fella."

"Not my fault you look the part."

"You sayin' you don't cotton to the way I look?" Her ears droop, their softness brushing my face.

I pretend my trousers aren't feeling a trifle confining. "Not at all, though you are a trifle manly."

Rising, squeezing my legs in hers, she plants a row of kisses up my muzzle. "Seems you need remindin' a' just how manly I ain't."

Paws working with a gunslinger's speed, she undoes her vest. We both blush, heat running through my whole body, save where I'm gripping the bottle. I set it down.

Reaching up, my wings explore her fur. Sandstone gives way to alabaster, sunlight blooming behind her. My world runs awash in pink and whites, sunlight streaming through her rose quartz ears like the heavens parting. She sighs, my breath is stolen, and I lose myself in them; those endlessly complex veins dragging me down, down, down, past the curve of her breasts to the slope of her hips as my wings trace up under the vest along her naked back.

As we get to kissing, I wonder how I'd ever thought the day was hot before now.

Chapter 6

"She's the Banana Spirit."

Boots crossed on the hearth, I watch the sheriff read in firelight. The expression on that foxy muzzle doesn't tell me much. Lawbat's more of a puzzle than I gave him credit for. I'm dreadful fond of the fool, so I ought to at least take a crack at solving the pretty little puzzle beside me.

I take a deep breath, stretching to make it look all easy and not like I'd been stewing it over in my head. "So tell me about bats."

Those delicate eyebrows rise from concentration to suspicion. "Bats?"

"Yeah. Ah mean, ah know ya cotton to songs and fruits and vests and such." I scratch my whiskers. "Just wonderin' what else there is to know."

Blake dips the book in his wing and looks at me askance. "Since when are you so interested in bat culture?"

"What?" I try to shrug off his concerns. His living room sits dark, the only light from a quiet little fire. The dim firelight plays along the carved grapevines in his matched chairs. "Ah'm already taken with one bat; stands to reason ah might find the rest agreeable."

He leans back and crosses his wings. "And this isn't a scheme to aid your thievery?"

"Why's everything gotta be a scheme?" My ears droop. I give him a glance sweet and warm as candied ginger. "What kind a' sheriff convicts a bun for a little innocent curiosity?"

"I am more familiar than most with your degree of innocence." The lawbat sets his novel on the table, interest sparkles like gold dust in those brown eyes. "I believe that makes me more of a character witness in this case."

My paw waves his words off. "Our business with the 'yote cave got me thinkin'…"

He crosses his wings. "I admit my concern has not abated."

"Ah asked the deputy about them, which uncorked a generous pour a' babble. Far as I could sort out, they're all keen on down instead of up." My paws dig a couple little scoops down at the air. "They see spirits and such as bein' deep down in the ground, right?"

"That is my understanding, yes."

"Well, hares spend spare moments lookin' up." A shrug rolls my shoulders against the back of the chair. "The more fearful sorts still trace out hungry monsters in the stars, but the most of us buns smile up at the moon rabbit."

Half a smile shines up his muzzle. "Moon rabbit?"

"We hares insist it's a hare, of course, but the name sticks." I nod up at the window, where a slice of night is visible through the blinds. "You've never noticed the pattern looks like a bunny?"

His pretty doe eyes trace the strip of sky. "No, but it wouldn't be the first bunny to sneak up on me."

I step to the window and throw aside the curtain I'm normally thankful for. "Come 'ere and look a second."

The lawbat stands up and breezes over.

I take him by the shoulders and point his fuzzy little muzzle up at the full moon. "See, she's got two ears goin' off to the left. Standing up over a mortar and pestle, or a witch's cauldron if you're of a hocus-pocus bend."

Riled up to the point of sass, he casts me back a smarmy smirk. "And that's how bunny ladies got so bewitching?"

My ears heat up like a desert noon. "Ya gonna let me tell mah story or just butter me up?"

He looks back out the window. "Please continue."

A tide of chatter tries to wash us on from my blush. "So ah figured: if bunnies and 'yotes think that different about things, how different are bats?"

"Well, we have at least a few points of commonality, many of which you've discovered." He nuzzles in at my neck.

I give a light chuckle, but don't let him shake my aim. "Ah'm being straight here, Jordan. You and I, we're on this road for the long haul, right?"

My pretty little bat leans back and studies my face. A sparkle more than mischief touches his eyes. "Yes." He winces and looks out the window in the hope I won't see him blink away the mist. "That is, I am if you are."

I clear my throat and steel myself against a tender tangle of feelings in my chest. "All that bein' the case, ah reckon it can't hurt to know a trifle more about each other. Where we come from and all that." I stiffen and look out the window too, heading off a haze in my own sight. "Might help me make sense a' yer batty tomfoolery."

Gentle wing fingers close around my paw. At the corner of my eye, his smile shines in the moonlight. "I'd like that very much."

⩘ ⸯ ⩘

We hop a train to Texas, which the lawbat tells me is the nearest place we can catch a true flying fox opera. The clattering passenger car's near to empty. The sheriff occupies himself reading a paperback somebody left on a seat. Some manner of weasel romance, he says, full of twists and furious action. Reminds him of a whole mess of stories I've never heard of.

When we run out of words, we watch the tiny civilized islands sweep by in the dusty vastness. Makes a bun think on the bigness of the world, seeing how long we can roll and still not be there. More than once, I've come near to falling asleep in the saddle, but the rattle and sway of a train is different from a pony.

As night falls, we fall into an unsteady sleep. I couldn't curl up with him in any properly improper way, lest some conductor walk in. Used his shortness to my advantage, though: leaning him against me so our heads don't whack together with every jostle of the train. Woke up using his wing as a blanket, so I guess there is some goodness in the world.

Stiff and sore, we stagger off the train and into the city. We heft our bags and walk through the crowded streets. As we leave the station behind, I puff little clouds of smoke. I never feel at home in a city. Too many pairs of eyes on me, so I can't just let my guard down. Back in the desert, I can bounce right out of town whenever I need a breather. Tires a bun out, being a stone-hard gunslinger. At least I can be something else when I'm alone, or alone with Blake. I clap a paw on his shoulder. "So where're we headin', sheriff?"

"The opera doesn't start until tonight." He checks his pocket watch.

"So we find a hotel and some foodstuffs. Then what?"

He fans the dust from my worn long coat. "I think we might be due for a little shopping."

☡ ☡ ☡

Dressed to the nines, Blake and I pay for our tickets and make our way into the concert hall. Electric lights burn in their blown-glass bubbles and brand little squiggles and scrawls on my vision. Grand arches sweep this way and that.

Various critters mill around in ace-high finery: tuxedo suits stuffed with ruffles, layer-cake dresses with shoulder poofs, and hats with feathers to rival my ears. A raccoon in a tailcoat chatters to his friends as we pass, a pastry in either paw.

I'm dressed in a smart little jacket that covers my womanly and weaponry assets. Combined with a silver-button vest and some new pants, I manage to look sharp without being useless. Even polished my boots for the occasion, after Blake's considerable fuss. I won't admit it, but doing so was probably for the best.

Lawbat's taken the excuse to drop all pretense of not dressing like a fruit salad. Every inch a member of the froufrou brigade, he's smattered with embroidery and sparkling with spangles. He's only wearing a waistcoat, rather than a jacket, as that's the bat fashion.

Everything's varnished wood and patterned drapery as we climb the stairs. I rest a paw on his pretty little shoulder. "What's the point in being a fella if ya dress as complicated as a lady anyhow?"

"I take pride in my appearance." He straightens the little vest, then turns a saucy eye my way. "You benefit from the same, when coerced into doing so."

A slight fluster prevents me from talking. Silly to get all namby-pamby over half a flattery, but I don't get heaped with praise for my looks too often. I take his wing on my arm. We must be a striking pair, were anybody looking. Which they aren't. I checked first.

The lawbat leads me up more than a few flights of stairs. Whoever built this place must've forgotten not everybody has wings. At last, we come to a sort of sitting room with curtained archways leading off it.

We reach our balcony and slip through the thick, whispering curtain. We're high enough that one bounce could take me to the chandelier. "Ah know this is a batty affair, but why'd ya get us seats in the clouds?"

He holds out the chair for me. "I felt a little privacy was called for."

"Blake, you cad!" Flopping onto the plush seat, I lean back at him for a grin. "You fixin' to take liberties with me in this little box?" My paw sweeps out at the other balconies, each seating a few innocent opera-goers. "You'll catch up on a lifetime's worth of scandalizing."

His ears shoot up. "Six! I'd never suggest such a thing!"

"Explains why ya need me around." I kick my boots up on the railing.

He gives them a dark look.

"What?" After a mumbly moment, I put them back on the floor. "Ya saw me clean 'em."

Curtains go up. Bunch of potted fruit trees poke up between painted wooden backgrounds. The band whips up into a bouncy tune.

A flutter of fruit bats blows onstage like loose leaves. They strut and swagger, dressed in clothes to outshine even the opera crowd. Going by their crowns, they're some kind of royal family. Thanks to the shape of the hall, I can hear their boast and babble, after a fashion. They take turns singing, but I haven't the faintest notion what.

My ears perk up straight, for all the good it does me. "Ah have no idea what these fools are sayin'."

He leans forward, his wing fingers on the balcony rail. "The lyrics are in Italian."

"They couldn't even be bothered to put the thing in English?" I har-rumph back into my seat. "Hope you're in a mood to be mah translator."

"I don't know Italian. Only Latin." He unfolds the pamphlet he got at the door.

I sputter and swing a paw open at the stage. "So we're just gonna sit here like a couple a' smiling lumps?"

"The point is to appreciate the music, the pageantry." He opens a leather case and pulls out a fancy little pair of binoculars.

"Field glasses?" I smirk. "We spyin' on the other boxes?"

"These, my good hare, are opera glasses." He offers them to me. "If you'd care for a better look."

I take the glasses and spy down at the actors. Gives me a fine view of their wild gesticulating. Then, through a puff of smoke, a sinister porcupine magician in a chili pepper hat turns up with a muzzle full of cackles. The royal family sings and squawks at him, but he does some manner of stomping dance and swishes a bunch of bright-colored ribbons at them.

The music goes all serious.

The porcupine sings a song. A skulk more flying foxes swoop in. These ones are draped in fiery colors. They dance and prance across the stage, bedeviling the royal family with pitchforks. Oh, and each pitchfork has little angry-looking chili peppers stuck on its tines.

I turn to the lawbat, exasperating fast. "What is even goin' on down there?"

"One of the defining operas of fruit bat canon."

I cross my arms. "More like somebody ate a bad fig and had a fever dream."

Blake cocks an eyebrow at me. "And now we see why a private box was necessary."

I cast an eye around the other balconies. All sorts of bats are watching the play like it makes any sense. Suppose Blake's right: they wouldn't take kindly to my not taking to their little song and dance.

On stage, half a dozen pint-sized bats bob out, dressed in round paper costumes painted pink, white, or black. They're each holding a sock full of dust that looks like smoke when whacked on something or someone.

With a held-back chuckle, I point down. "One way to keep the little brats out of trouble: dress 'em up like a piñata."

"They're the peppercorn devils." His fingertip traces down the printed list of characters. "Lesser demons in the service of Pfeffer, the wicked spice sorcerer."

For all their impressive tongues, fruit bat culture doesn't make a lick of sense. I fight a knock-out battle inside not to let word slip.

The royal bats fly up to a painted wood tower and start dumping buckets of blue rags on their tormentors. The assorted devils just stamp about and wave their pitchforks. Two peppercorns knock into each other and tip over, but do an honest job of trying to look scary from the floor. More songs shore up this part of the production.

I borrow the pamphlet long enough to read about how the whole stage is meant to bounce echolocation chirps just right. Even has some manner of fooling bats into thinking someone's there when they're not. That seems like the regular job of an echo, and being a bunny the refinement of various squeaks are lost on me. A flowery burst of fiddles draws my attention back to the stage.

A new actor sways in, darn near taller than the scenery. She's bundled in yellow silks and dabbed with green dye. Of course, she's trumpeting a heroic song.

I lean in to Blake. "Why's that giraffe all painted up like a banana?"

"She's the Banana Spirit." How he says these things with a serious face, I'll never know. He gives me a look, then prods the pamphlet at me. "The cast list is right here."

While I'm sure it is, taking it from the lawbat just now is more than my prickly pride can bear. I feel thorny at being baffled by this fever dream of an opera, doubly so for knowing the fault's all mine. I ran a thousand miles to get away from all this high-class humbuggery, only to sally forth back into it with all the sense of a March hare. Maybe I should've soaked up a little more culture while I could, before blowing away like a dust bunny to the desert. Can't reckon why the lawbat puts up with my lack of refinement.

A touch graces my paw. Jordan's fingers curl around mine. He smiles, then leads my gaze with his back to the play.

I squirm atop a pile of troublesome feelings, then brace myself and dare to look back at the battiness below.

Below us, the Banana Spirit weaves a wobbly dance, hooves clacking onstage, spreading a squabble among the chili peppers. Or possibly a consternation. Either way, she keeps on crooning. The small army of peppers make moves to prod her with their pitchforks, but the towering lady swats them away.

The evil magician starts on a song of his own, but ends up getting banished. Without a pause, the royal bats flutter down from their tower for a spritely dance with the Banana Spirit. And another song.

Long after the curtain drops and the fruit bats finish their flutters of applause, I sit there staring. "What'd ah just watch?"

"Intrusi Piccanti." Lawbat flashes the pamphlet at me, which has the name.

I narrow my eyes at him, like this has all been some kind of joke. "Don't tell me that's the whole shebang."

Blake's studying me, amused. "It is."

I pat his shapely little shoulder and surrender. "Take pity on mah folksy bumpkinery."

"The opera's from the late 1600s, when a new wave of spicy peppers were introduced to the Mediterranean." He swoops a wing at the stage. "The influx caused a culinary revolution and many fruit bats weren't ready for it. Until ways of balancing out the piquant flavors were discovered, the peppers were seen as a menace."

"Y'all were oppressed by peppers?" I laugh a little. "Yer more tender than ah thought."

"Two hundred years hence, I have little trouble with peppers." Blake puffs up. The opera has left him proud and extra fancy. "You, on the other wing, "

My gaze drifts back down to the stage, as if it had any answers. The audience files out, already yammering about what a fine opera it was and how much sense it made. I can hear them walking past our curtains as they chatter toward the stairs.

🦇 〽 🦇

"Now here's some bat culture ah can take in." I lift the teacup to my lips, blowing at the steam.

The hotel room around us is small but stuffed with finery. Lace curtains sway at the open window. The fireplace is scuffed and singed, but scrubbed newly clean. Patterns swirl under my fingers on the padded armchair. The table between me and the lawbat is delicate, but proud: not unlike the lawbat himself.

"Fine black tea from the Orient..." With a tilt of his wing, Blake poured himself a cup of Earl Grey tea. "...with the peel of the deadly

Bergamot orange."

I spy down into my cup at the tea leaves, but conclude the sheriff isn't keen to poison me. "Who ever heard of a poison orange?"

He folds up into his chair, his muzzle right over the tea. "Who ever heard of a bunny gunfighter?"

"You may have a point, lawbat." I sip at the tea. Still hot enough to hurt, but too good to wait for. The opera offers me a lot to think back on, but runs short on much I actually learned. Reckon it'll take quite a number of days with the lawbat to get to know him right. Don't mind terribly, seeing as those days come with nights.

Only when Blake squirmed under my gaze did I realize how wanton I'd let it get. As I took another sip of tea, I decided I didn't mind that terribly either.

Chapter 7

I smash it out of the air, splattering it into blue goo.

I land a boot on Cur Johnson's muzzle. He spins away, howling.

The rest of the Pine City Gang close on me, razor grins gleaming.

Last time I do the lawbat a favor.

My boots crunch gravel. I spring into the air, twirling cork-screw fashion. My Colts flash like steel lightning in my paws. Dirt explodes below me, driving back the fistful of highwaymen. Two bounces later, I'm standing atop the stolen Wells Fargo stagecoach. The team of ponies neigh and buck, all flustered, ready to bolt. Can't say as I blame them.

A masked bandito trains his rifle on me.

Sheriff Jordan Blake swoops down like the cloak of night, snatching the rifle from the flabbergasted pine marten. He tosses the iron my way.

Flipping one pistol back into a holster, I catch it— Winchester '73, and not well cared for. Pity I don't have time to steal the bullets. "Good thing ya asked 'em to surrender, sugarwings." I wallop a rat with the stock for climbing up toward me. "Workin' out right well."

The lawbat dives behind the stage as Cur Johnson's men set the air boiling with gunfire. "Hardly the time —huh!— for your irreverence, Six!" His back's to the varnished wood of the coach.

The weight of an echo pulls my silver gun down. I drop, bullets screaming by my ears. They nick one of those and this bunny'll introduce them to all manner of unpleasantness.

The pistol in my right paw hums again with echo. I fire, without looking, around the front of the wagon.

Splinters shower my arm. I shake them from my fur, checking for blood. Must have hit part of—

The stagecoach rumbles under me. Shit. I look up to see the team of

ponies racing off with the splintered half of a hitch. I look behind me, down the hill. "Blake…"

"Still not the time, Six!" He's reloading that little Schofield pistol, blind to the fact his cover's leaving.

The gunfire hangs. Powder smoke hangs in the air, making my nose twitch.

Cur Johnson and his men watch, slack-muzzled, as their stolen stagecoach departs.

I could, by rights, plug them all right now, but they let the coach crew go when they stole the thing. What's more, I got thirty yards before I run outta mesa.

Blake snaps the cylinder back down into his gun and turns, coming eye to eye with the Pine City Pine Martens. They share a silent moment as I rumble away, rolling fast under the weight of the gold bars in its belly.

"Stop the coach!" Cur Johnson barks at his gang then unloads at Blake, who's scrambling behind a rock pile.

As one, the pine martens give chase after my stage. I'm lying on my belly, reaching for the brake. Whenever I get close, of course, Cur shoots at me again. Gritting back the bunny urge to freeze, I holler: "You figure killin' me's gonna stop this thing?!" I get the trigger-happy varmint in my sights, but the coach jolts on a stone and my shot goes wild. "Damnation!"

The shot spooks him good, though. He dives for cover, letting Blake scamper out from his own and take to wing after me. Dandy— he'll have a bat's eye view to my plummet.

The cliff's mighty close now. Dust swirls up from the sheer drop off. Arizona heat fingers through my fur.

I coil back to jump into the clot of bandits. It'll be a nasty tussle, but—

A bullet cracks past my ear.

I tremble, bunny instinct freezing me a moment. Turns out to be a moment I don't have.

A stab of plummet, then a crash. My hat slips free of my ears, twisting on the wind.

The back wheels spin on empty air. I scramble for purchase. The belly of the stage grinds against the cliff edge, pitching backward. As the front end pitches skyward, I glimpse Blake's wing beating over the heads of the banditos, a desperate glint in his gold-flecked eyes.

My hat settles on the cliffside, all peaceable.

I tumble through air, falling with the wagon. The rifle floats up past me. Shame the last thing I'll ever see'll be that rusted Winchester. Always figured if I died looking at a gun, a fella'd be holding it, though.

My gut and the horizon do flips. My heart drums above a taut nausea. Ground's coming at me in a hurry. I close my eyes and breathe: "Jordan, I love you—"

A painful grip crushes on my boot.

I'm yanked upward.

"What in blue blazes?!" I open tear-stung eyes to see my leg dangling in the lawbat's hind paws. "Jordan, you sonovabitch!"

"You're welcome." He flaps like a poster in a cyclone. The stagecoach crashes against the cliff face.

My guts jockey for position. My ears dangle into the nothing. "Ahh!" I curl upward, grabbing at his ankles. "Don't go droppin' me!"

"I won't." The fruit bat's steel grasp tightens. He eases into a glide, sailing us around the corner of the mesa. "You're madder than the March hare, you know that?"

I watch across the gulf as the gang scatters like shed fur into the desert. "That's a trifle unfair, lawbat." Chasing my breath, I cough half a desert's worth of dust. "It bein' June an' all." I glance back at the cliff, catching little glimmers down its side. My tail twitches. "So that reward's for those pretty gold bars, right?"

⊻ ⋊ ⊻

Gold bar's a weighty thing.

Sunset simmers at the lip of the canyon high above. Shadows grow fast and deep around my boots. One of the shreds of sunlight slithers across another bar, standing half-buried in dry earth. I pull out and heft it. It's almost too smooth to grip, even with gloves over my fluffy hands. Dirt trails off, a thin whisper in the shadows.

The valley floor is peppered with deep little gullies. I've seen saloon floors with fewer holes, though the lawbat has asked me to stop blasting new holes in the ones in his town. My ears rise at a slight crackle in the air. Can't find a source for it, though. Canyon like this does funny things to the sound of Blake building a fire. Air chilling fast, and fruit bats don't have the thick fur us hares do.

I watch the lawbat toss another section of wagon wheel onto the hungry flames. The ruined wagon slumps behind him, though parts of it lay scattered up the cliffside and around us. Pity the strongbox broke open—I wouldn't have spent the last hour picking up loose change. "Ah've never missed so much in all my life, havin' only one of mah daddy's guns."

"I wasn't going to bring it up." He scans the lip of the cliffside again, ears perked for a return by the bandits. "Guess you'll have to practice like the rest of us." His smile is consolation for the sass, badge glimmering in the firelight.

I check my replacement gun with only a little resentment, then look to the lawbat. "You don't regret letting those bandits go?"

He shakes his muzzle. "They haven't killed anybody, as far as I'm aware. We don't have the manpower to detain them and it strikes me as unjust to fly ahead and wait in deadly ambush."

I smirk. Charitable for crooks who were trying to plug us an hour ago. "He'd have liked you." I stand beside him, watching the fire. "My daddy, that is."

That foxish muzzle tilts up at me. "Is that so?"

"Yer upright and ya don't lord it over folk." Ears down, I catch him looking from the corner of my eye. "He liked that."

"I don't know if I've ever been paid so high a compliment." His wing fingers take my paw.

Blushing, I hold his grasp for a moment. I mull over telling him more, but I can't think of anything that doesn't seem mawkish. Instead, in the dying light, I polish the bar up a bit with the side of my paw, then reflect on my reflection. A trifle dented up, but still pure gold. Walking back to him, I strike a pose with the gold, waggling it up by my nose so it shines in the firelight. "You sure there's no way ah could convince you to fly me and the gold outta here?"

He pokes the fire with a section of broken spoke. "Much as I'd enjoy the convincing, I can't fly carrying both you and a hundred pounds of gold."

I set the newest bar into a satchel with three others, close the bag with care, then strain to lift it. Rips straight through. The bars stay exactly where they are. "Ah! Ya may have a point." I sigh and straighten to meet his fire-lit eyes. "Suppose we ought to leave directly."

The lawbat smirks. "I can fly and see in the dark. Can you keep from falling down one of these gullies? Or the cliff again?"

"For that much gold, ah'd learn to fly." I spy up the darkened cliff, then check my revolvers. I beat the tar out of the pine marten bandits and Blake swore his deputy carted them all back to town, but luck loves to shortchange me. Could be they have friends. "Don't suppose ya have more bullets?"

His sleek little muzzle gets an annoyed look. "You may recall you stole mine before the shootout began."

"Ah, right."

The bat leans back against the shattered wagon's side and tosses me my hat, which he kindly recovered from the top of the cliff. "You realize you'll someday be the death of us."

As I tug it over my ears, a dollop of sass heaps onto my words. "We're still livin'. And ah helped you recover stolen goods."

"All of it?" He cocks an eyebrow at me.

I flash him a charming smile. "Be a crime to give it all back."

He groans and kicks a chunk of wagon into the fire. "What else did you pillage from the wreckage?"

I take on airs and graces, turning my nose up at his suggestion. "Ah shan't be compelled to testify against mahself."

"Fifth Amendment wasn't intended to help you bamboozle your lover, Six."

My ears blaze at the word. I cover my shyness with a low chuckle. "Guess you'll have to make a thorough search of mah person."

The flying fox bites back his shock at my suggestion. He crosses his wings and plays at being unflappable. "I just may."

"Don't make a bun a promise..." I step right up and tip his muzzle to mine. "...if ya don't plan to keep it."

He smiles, eyes shining, and gives me a little kiss. "The reward will have to suffice."

I cast a glance to the gold, sitting on that ripped-out bag. "With this much money, a bun wouldn't have to play outlaw to live however she wants."

Taking a seat by the fire, he shakes his head. "As an agent of the law, I can verify it doesn't work that way."

A little snap of anger flares up, charring the sweet little moment we'd been having. "Ah've seen it work that way more 'an a few times."

Blake puffs himself up with resolution. "Stealing it would make us no better than the original thieves."

"Lucky for me, ah have my own personal lawbat, ready to lock me up." My muzzle tightens with agitation, teeth clenched.

"Is there another way to get you to hold still for five minutes?"

I sit down by the fire and have myself a little sulk. "Could always come along when ah go. Show me you lov—that I matter." I watch the flames for a moment, waiting for him to answer. "Blake?"

He looks at darkness with an ears-up silence.

I listen too, but my ears still haven't forgiven me for the day's gunfire. All I hear is the wind through the canyon and the crackle of the fire. A faint tingle traces through my father's gun, setting me on edge.

Blake jumps up. A scorpion long as my forearm crawls up on the rock he'd been seated on.

I draw iron, fan the hammer, and blast the critter in half. Dark blue slime streaks in a fine spray against the rocks. I swing my silver gun skyward with a wisp of powder smoke, watching for more. "Ah think ah know where we are. We need to leave."

Fool lawbat kneels to look over the gooey, twitching remains "What was this?"

I cock my next round, then draw that the blue steel one too. No time to be picky. "King scorpion."

The sheriff stands. His lithe little body stiffens with concern. "They always invite themselves to parties?"

On light paws, I move toward the gold, guns out. "Starved or startled, by mah guess. Not supposed to come after folk."

In the cool desert night, we freeze, ears up. Skittering rises all around. Half a dozen scorpions, the same size, scurry toward us from all sides.

I open up with both guns, shredding the group to dark shiny smears. The sound of each shot whip-cracks down the canyon.

He squeaks with alarm.

Hare instincts whisper a chill to my blood, urging me to leave. For once, I agree. "We'd best run."

More skitters and scrambles echo beyond the firelight.

Breathing hard, I swallow and resolve myself to a long, hard run down the canyon. "Take the gold. Ah'll be fine."

With a single flap, he hops onto a rock. He's almost eye-level with me. "What?!"

I thumb back the hammers on both my revolvers. "In no mood to debate, lawbat. Fly."

A dozen more scorpions, at least as big, scuttle from the darkness. A few small ones too.

I kick the campfire, scattering it in wide arc. Hunks of burning wood bounce through the mess of spines and stingers.

Dancing around the flames, the scorpions overrun our little campsite.

Seeing Blake struck dumb, I holster and bounce away with the gold. Scorpion shadows, tall as a man, tangle and twist along the canyon walls, projected by firelight. I waste no time in hightailing it through the burning wood.

The bat swoops after me. "Drop the gold, you daft bunny!"

Hugging the gold to my chest, every bounce threatens to knock it from my grasp. My running boots smash down on a few scorpions. "No!"

A sudden scrape at my feet snags my attention. I glance down to find two latched onto my boots. With a spirited dance, I kick them loose. Those claws leave deep, fresh scratches on the leather.

Lawbat grabs my shoulders with his feet. Dust whips by me in a desperate flutter. But try as he might, he can't take off.

Tightening my grip on the gold bars, I pick off two plate-size scorpions who tried to cut into my path. They fold wrong-way-out, legs flying in all directions. A third one jumps from a rock and latches to my boot. I reward him with a swift kick against the same rock.

At all once, I make it clear of them. The clicks and scuttles fade to quiet behind me.

A whole mess of the buggers pop up in front of me, waving sharp claws in the moonlight. I bounce again. The toe of my boot catches on a rock and sends me stumbling. All four gold bars fly from my grasp.

The gold crunches to the dry dirt and slides under a large rock, just inside a den of more scorpions. Lots more. They scamper right on top of the bars, daring me to reach in with quivering tails.

Still on hands and knees, I give the bugs a glare with more venom than they could ever hope for. I stand, drawing my second gun. I level both guns at the cave. Both guns click, empty. I flip both around to grip the barrels.

"Six…" Blake calls my name with such concern that I look up from my fury.

Hand-size claws rise from the rock. Starlight gleams off its many eyes, glinting through endless rows of hairs. The big scorpion leaps off the top of the den at me.

I smash it out of the air, splattering it into blue goo.

Scorpions rush from the den and from all sides. I jump off the top of the den, smashing more of them under my boots. Free from the weight of the gold, I bounce up the side of the cliff. Blake, gripping hard on my shoulders, spreads his wings. We fly off as unending hordes of the creatures slash their claws and tails after us.

🌙 ☄ 🌙

A pretty sunrise lights the next morning, painting the sky and mesas a rich spread of colors. Long, thin clouds catch the sunshine above, adding to the cheery picture. Shaping up to be a dandy day.

I sulk on the edge of the cliff, empty revolvers in my paws. I swear I can see a faint glimmer of gold at the base of the cliff. Barefoot steps behind me tell of the fruit bat pacing near. I grumble. "I still say ya could swoop in and nab the bars one at a time."

He stands beside me, heedless of the edge. Guess wings do that for a fella. "And stick my foot in a nest of scorpions?"

My ears are down, having not heard a scorpion in hours. Stagecoach tracks lead off the edge beside me, with the smashed coach itself far below. A thin ribbon of smoke rises from our fire beside it. "Ah'm liable to douse the whole mess in kerosene. That'd teach 'em."

Lawbat scoffs. "Once it cooled enough for us to reach the gold, the surviving scorpions could too. Unless you're planning to burn the whole valley?"

I look up at him from under the brim of my hat. "Outta principle, you understand."

Squatting so his toes dangle off the cliff, he lands a wing-hand on my shoulder. "On the bright side, we're still living."

I'm still irked, but he tricks me into a smile. "That's rich, lawbat." I spit off the edge of the cliff. "We'll get ya a pair of oven mitts—no, you can't grip the bars like that. Maybe a diving suit…"

He crosses his wings. "Or we could wait until noon, when the scorpions retreat to their holes, then fish out the gold with a stick."

Resigned, I wiggle my whiskers. "Could do that, I suppose."

"You realize we have to give the gold back."

I perk an ear at him. "What if we didn't 'find' the gold?"

"No, Six." His badge shines bright in the morning light.

"Fine, fine." Holstering my guns, I stand. "Yeah, ah reckon you're right."

"Surprised you didn't put up more of a fight."

Patting him on shoulder, I shove a gold bar further into my pocket. "You must be a good influence on me. Let's head back—I'll buy ya breakfast." Out of his sight, I touch the gold brick I managed to snag.

Chapter 8

"He's a slight little thing, and sensitive. Got all kinds of poetical inclinations."

Lawbat's dear and all, but he leaves a bit to be desired when it comes to explaining his culture. I could hound the boy with questions, but I have this aversion to admitting I don't know things. Besides, the fluttery fool's possessed of a bran-like surplus of moral fiber.

To clear my head, I headed to Prescott. Nice enough place, when it's not burning down, but not so nice that folk give you a side-eye for carrying a little iron. Town may have lost being the territory capital twice, but it has some ace-high shops: general stores, drug stores, and the like. On a lark, I wander into a dress shop.

It's not the first time, though I don't make a habit of bringing this up to Blake. I just want to figure out what ladies see in wearing the things. Often, some sales clerk will come bustling up and try to sell me on a dress for my "lady." Though the notion of seeing the lawbat in a dress again tickles me, I fear he'd get a get a mite thorny if I ambushed him with one store-bought.

The door chimes open. In breezes a fruit bat in a dandelion dress, decked with puffery, lace, and poofy mustard sleeves. The sleeves are fake, just little drapes hanging down her shoulders. Anything more would get in the way of flight, I know from Blake. She drifts through the racks, graceful as a leaf, wings glowing in the light. Her golden eyes swoop over the wares.

An idea takes root in my mind: maybe this lady could give me the rundown on bat culture. Might help in my aim to have Blake make any kind of sense. Can't just saunter over there and say "ah'm keen on this bat, ya see..." That's a sure route to getting slapped when you're dressed as a fella.

My gaze tracks over to a row of dresses. Well, if clothes are the only thing stopping me, that's easy enough to remedy.

I grab a dress. Some simple affair, like a farmer would wear. I double-check it's free of laces or impossible buttons, then sneak back to the dressing booth. I'm halfway out of my gunbelt before I realize what I'm doing would please my relations back East. I change anyhow. I try to clomp out of my boots in ladylike manner, so as not to draw the storekeeper over.

Once I hop into the dress, I stuff my belongings into my satchel and bounce out of the booth and look around. I don't see her. For once, I wish I was taller, tall enough to see a short little bat between these rows of dresses and other finery. My ears rise to the challenge, sweeping the store—

"Excuse me, ma'am?"

I spring straight into the air, whack my head on the ceiling, and land with a thump. "Glad sakes!" I rub my battered skull. "Ya mind not sneakin' up on a bun so?"

"Sorry! Are you alright?" The bat herself stands before me. Of course. "I was just going to ask if you were waiting for someone."

My paws try to settle on a gunbelt that's not there. I play it off as propping them on my slim hips. "Don't trouble yerself over it. We hares're a high-strung sort." I clear my throat of its usual gruff and gravel. "Ah'm not waitin' on anybody in particular, just life in general. Thought ah'd do a little shopping to fill the time." That's not a lie, if I'm honest.

"Ah." She crosses her wings and looks up and down my present get up. "No special events coming up that would require a new outfit?"

"None, which is a touch unfortunate." I blink, unsure if I meant that last. "Least, unless ya have a notion."

"How's that?"

"Ah'm actually courtin'— Er, bein' courted." Must admit I'm a little rusty at talking like a lady.

She tilts her foxy muzzle up into a laugh. "A modern lady can do some courting. I've seen it."

"Yeah." I push past the rust and rattle on. "Would be open to any notions, if you've got 'em. He's flying fox, and a sheriff besides."

"Well! Aren't you lucky." Her muzzle alights with delight.

I blush furiously. If she's getting at where his batty tongue's been getting at, I may have to reconsider my stance on hitting women. "O-oh?"

"Why yes! Not many of us out this way." Her wing lifts toward the window. "Not the ideal climate for fruit."

"Yeah, he keeps the tinned fruit companies in business." I roll my eyes. "Oughta see what the boy can do to a jar of peaches." Gotta get my mind clear of this territory; last thing I need right now's an image of the lawbat with a sticky muzzle.

Amusement sails across her muzzle. "Well, what's he like?"

"He's a slight little thing, and sensitive. Got all kinds of poetical inclinations."

"Oooh, an artist and a lawman." She crosses her wings, leaning in with interest.

"To the manner born. Causes me no end a' grief." I sigh, smiling in spite of myself. "But he's loyal and fond of me. Does his sheriffing out in White Rock, though. "

"You ever consider taking him to the nectar bee?" She taps a wing finger on her arm. "Haven't met a fruit bat yet who'd object."

"The what now?"

"Nectar bee. You know." She does a little sway, that patterned dress shimmers in the window light.

I lift an ear. "'Fraid I don't."

"They're a fruit bat gathering. Started as a way of preparing fruits for winemaking, but machinery takes care of that part now." Her laugh is sweet and high as a peach out of reach. "These days, it's more of an excuse to sample excellent vintages and exotic fruits. Between the two of them, it becomes exceptionally easy to buy more than you mean to."

A scoff escapes my muzzle. "A batty event if ever I've heard of one."

She smiles sweetly. "I'm Clementine, by the way."

I smile back, trying not to show my nerves. "S— So nice to meet you." I shake her wing. My first name sticks in my throat after long years of not saying it aloud. "Miss Haus."

"Well, Ms. Haus, I was going to get a coffee." She tilts her head toward the door. "Would you care to join me?"

"Just let me pay off mah tab here." I saunter up to the till, dig my wallet out of the overstuffed satchel, and plunk down the cash in front of a surprised feline shopkeeper. Legally in possession of my getup, I follow her across the street. Every step sends a little gust of wind up my legs, which is a trifle scandalizing. Now and again, sharp little rocks also poke at my bare paws, which is plain bothersome.

We get to a little cafe. Little across, but tall. Roasting coffee enriches the air. A selection of kettles rattle and puff behind the counter. In the back, a giraffe clatters cups onto high shelves.

A second giraffe stilts over. His apron hangs like a banner, emblazoned with bleached coffee stains. "Welcome." His accent is deep and rich. "What can I get you ladies?"

Her wings steeple with refinement. "Just a coffee. I'll add my own cream and sugar, if you please."

Somewhere near the ceiling, he nodded. "And for you, madam?"

I wink up at him. "Black as a moonless night."

He huffs. Whether it's at my wit or his weariness, I can't discern. How any woman has time to care what anybody thinks while managing all the frills and fittings of a typical dress I may never know. I'd take it as a success in life if I never find out.

She fans a wing over her steaming drink. "So, are you a local?"

"Ah'm not a local to anywhere." I drop my satchel beside the chair. It lands with a thump of boots. "Bounced between here and back East." I endeavor to sit like something other than a saddle-sore cowboy. Feels unnatural to have my ankles crossed and knees together.

"You do seem to have…layers of culture." A smile brightens her dark muzzle. "Characteristic of a woman who's lived all over. Worldly, I suppose is the word."

My heart gets a chill whenever she brings up my womanliness. I flip an ear to hide my discomfort. "Mah world has consisted of White Rock more and more."

A glimmer of amusement shines in her eyes. "A charming suitor will do that."

My polite laugh sounds only a little like gravel grinding. It's been a long time since my mother and grandmother tried to straighten me into a proper lady and now I'm struggling to recall the lessons. Who'd have figured it'd be useful after all? At least they won't find out.

Our coffees arrive, along with a mismatched sugar bowl and creamer.

Clementine adds both until her drink's one egg shy of a custard.

With admirable grit, I lift the cup in a delicate and grace manner. Pinky out and fingers back from the rim, so as to not to tempt tea into soaking in. Teacups aren't that great an imposition; we bunnies are always thankful for handles, seeing as we have fur over our paw pads. More than one shot glass has fired out of my grasp, especially if it's not the first of the evening.

"Have you given the nectar bee any thought? It's nearly a month out." She flashes a conspiratorial look. "One must give gentlemen time to prepare for such things, after all. They're such creatures of routine."

"Oh, ah'll have to give the matter some contemplating." I slap the table a little harder than is strictly ladylike.

She leans back a little in her chair, while still keeping perfect posture. "I'll be in attendance too, if you want a tour."

"That'd be mighty kind of yew." I nod. "Though ah must confess ah wouldn't know what to wear. Never had cause to get into flying fox fashion."

"Oh, I'm sure we could find something suitable." Her wing fingers spread, as if she's already imagining me hustling into a bustle. "Just avoid the lace suspenders—they're passé now, no matter what the boutique owners say."

I smile, aware I'm now cornered into buying two dresses in a day. That's two more than I've bought in the last twenty-odd years. This distresses me some, but it's all part of the plan.

Chapter 9

"Tickles somethin' fierce."

I slip inside the hotel and tip my hat to the proprietor. Evening light bathes the rough wooden walls. As I climb the stairs, I'm followed by unfamiliar voices and the clatter of ponies outside. My shadow soars ahead, down the hall to where I find my small room.

Cigarette smoke wafts out. Some fool must have left the window open— anything could drift in. I step inside.

The shades are drawn on the room's only window. Scraps of light stretch over the nightstand and along the narrow bed. A form lounges on it. Before I can even call out, I spot the ample ears of a desert hare and the ready Colts of a gunslinger.

"Six!"

"Lawbat." She lifts her hat in greeting. The remains of a few cigarettes adorn the nightstand as their ghosts haunt the air.

I glance back through the door, then close it, whispering: "What're you doing here?"

"Unquietin' your life, is all." She crosses her booted ankles atop my bed.

"You knew this was my hotel room?"

"Had mahself a little look-see at the ledger." Her ears drop; my pulse rises. Her muzzle breaks into a pout. "You're not keen on seein' me?"

I brush a wing under her chin. "I wouldn't say that…"

Smiles sneak up on the both of us as we put our muzzles to good use. I'm drawn to her, knees on the bed. It's been weeks since I last saw her. Feels like years.

She pulls me forward into her strong arms, gentle paws stroking my wings. The feathery smoothness of her fur traces through the fuzz there, calling to mind soft winds and intimate encounters. Her blue eyes gaze down like stormy skies. Her beauty dawns like the Arizona sunrise. "Keep lookin' at a bunny like that and she's liable think yew missed her."

"Nonsense." I get back to kissing her hello; tobacco lingers on her mouth. Almost enough to make a bat enjoy that taste. Almost.

"Just sayin'." Her paws venture under my vest, exploring the fur of my back as I do the same to her stomach.

Noise outside— hooting and hollering. Nothing close, but her fancy ears rise. She smirks as I watch and inclines her head toward the noise. "Reckon as sheriff you're obliged to see about that disturbance."

"It's not in my jurisdiction, Six." I nuzzle the dangling tip of one ear. "I'm only in town to testify."

"Ya did that, and Hayes' personal banditos are getting shipped off to jail." Her paws caress my shoulder blades. Each claw trails through my fur to scritch along the skin beneath; my muzzle tilts upward of its own accord at this treatment. "Yer pretty at ease in a courtroom."

"It is my old haunt." I trace my wing fingers through her fluffy tail. "Perhaps I ought to take a brief hiatus to do some legal consulting."

"Even a fruit bat needs a nest egg." Her lightning eyes flash to the window, then to me. "Let's see what the ruckus is about." Another kiss, between my ears this time. "Maybe bend an elbow at the bar."

"I don't take to drinking." I lean in. Her chest fur warms my cheek. My muzzle rests on her modest breasts.

"But ah take to you, and maybe a nip a' something'd loosen ya up."

My body aches for her from ears to toes. "I don't need loosening up—"

"Hush now." The hare puts a finger to my lips. "Matter's settled. Hare's discretion."

I sigh against her, rueful.

She leans in, her lips against my ear. "Promise ah'll make it worth the while."

Tingles shiver down my body like rain. "That so?"

"Mmmmhmmm." She drifts off me like a cloud, leaving me with a smile. Only after she's gone do I realize half a dozen bullets vanished off my belt. Show-off. She snags a wrapped parcel off the table and turns to regard me, clutching it to her chest. "Close yer eyes."

I comply. As usual, I am left to wonder what kind of plan she has.

Turns out, I don't have to wonder long. Moments later, she calls out: "Okay, you can look now."

My thief stands before me.

In a dress.

A dress. Violet fabric blooms around her, a shade before daybreak. Silver buttons glisten down her chest and stomach, almost as bright as the gun she still carries. The gunbelt's slung around her waist, accenting her hips as the dress sweeps downward. Rough boots and trousers show at the hem, assuring me I don't have the wrong bunny.

Feeling faint, I grip the doorframe.

Six steadies me by the waist. "Nobody catches wind a' this. Ever." Blue eyes smolder down from between demure ears. "Comprende?"

I squeak. My ears have no doubt turned seven different shades of pink by now.

"Good. Come on now." Her paw closes on my wing thumbs. "We've got ourselves a fandango to see to."

☟ ☪ ☟

It's a stag dance. We don't have them in White Rock. Too few stags. But I've heard of them.

The ratio of menfolk to the fairer sex out west runs something like four to one, precluding typical dances. A stag dance is the Frontier remedy: men get together and dance with each other, often in dresses. I'll spare you the cruder rumors as to why the deer host these; we'll just say they happen most in the fall.

Still can't look Six straight on. Just too surreal, even from the corner of my eye. She drags me onto the dance floor, twirling me to the yowl of the fiddle and clatter of hoofbeats. Sawdust kicks up from the bar floor. I'm blushing to the fur whenever Six locks eyes. She just laughs, lost to the moment. I try to keep up with her and manage only to step on my bare hind paws a few times.

As songs wear on, other fellows trade off partners, but Six's eyes makes it clear I'm taken, only letting me go during line dances. Not that

I'd prefer to dance with some lonesome buck. Bawdy limericks and bois-terous cheering pepper the evening. Six is the only woman, of course. No lady would be seen in a saloon, unless she wanted a reputation as a "public woman." That said, they'd have to guess she was a woman first. Even in a dress, she makes a better man than most folks present.

The music slows. Nestled in the anonymity of the crowd, I rest my head against her chest a moment. She responds in kind, resting her head on my ears. In the midst of the music, in the mist of the moment, I am tempted into fantasy. Then I remember where we are and how indecent this must look, and that her paws lay a trifle low on my waist.

I straighten, whispering. "Six, restrain yourself."

"Ah am." A scoundrel's wink. "Were I not, ah'd haul ya over the bar and take ya in a womanly fashion."

Shock paints my face. What a thing to say! And in public!

"Oh, fix yer muzzle." My thief scoffs, sounding almost male again. "Like you ain't a party to the event."

"I'll thank you not to scandalize me further, ma'am." I tip her into a slow spin on my wing. That violet dress twirls around her with elegance. We make a decent pair when she's not stomping all over the place. Pity we couldn't do this back in White Rock, even if we had the dances.

"Shame ah couldn't get you a dress." Her eyes catch mine, full of mischief. "Again." She twirls back into my wings, squeezing my hip. "We both know ya got the figure."

Heat races through my wings. "Don't say that."

A buck and wolf stagger past us. Tipsy flourishes reveal their fond-ness for waltzing past the bar. They plow through the crowd, antlers first.

Six suppresses a laugh, watching them go, ears flopping against my face.

I smirk. "Looks to be more than just us enjoying ourselves."

"You reckon we might go enjoy ourselves a trifle more privately?"

Before I can reply, shouting draws my attention— a pang of discord cutting through the revelry. I turn.

Two bucks loom over an ocelot waiter. The bigger one has the scrawny cat by the apron, whiskey dripping off the both of them. The second white-tail staggers up, stabbing a thick-nailed finger at the frantically apologizing feline. The music staggers and stops.

"Is there a problem here?" An empty shot glass rolls against my bare hind paw.

"None a' your concern, batty."

"Afraid I have to disagree." I adjust my badge, letting it glint in the lantern light.

Folks clear back, forming a ring around the deer and me. Both bucks level a steel gaze at me. The big one laughs, hot whiskey breath washing over my face. "You ain't the sheriff here."

"Quite correct." I feel my years of law school sneaking up on me. "But your sheriff wouldn't be too pleased if I let mayhem descend on his town."

A crackle of tension runs through the crowd. The deer stare me down.

His wings spread in an amiable manner. "Besides, I'm sure our spotted garçon is eager to bring you a free round."

The ocelot mews in agreement.

"There. Seems to me you've got every reason to be reasonable." Smiling as one hind paw caresses my gun, I wait for their response.

Six smirks at me, having seen this play before.

The big deer's paw releases, leaving impressions on the cat's apron. He sneers. "Better be the good stuff, or we'll have ourselves some trouble."

Tail wrapped around himself, the feline pads back to the bar in a spotted flash.

I wait to see the drinks delivered, the smaller deer moving to flank me. I don't back down an inch, waiting until the fine cervines have their drinks in hand before I declare the matter settled. The band cobbles a song back together as I walk back to my thief.

"Nice talkin', lawbat." She tips her hat. "Though ya could've gotten me a whiskey in the bargain."

"You've always got to push your luck, don't you?" I tap her boot with my toe. "Can't just be content that I adopted your method of defusing bar brawls?"

"Ah could be made more content." She gets that scoundrel smile. "Care to see about that privacy we spoke on?"

My own muzzle mirrors it. "I feared you would never ask."

I let my gaze slip over the deer to see they've stopped hassling the help. We rise from our table and pick our way through the crowd, Six breaking off for a customary shot of whiskey "for luck" and emerging with a half bottle.

"That's a lot of luck."

"I aim to get luckier." She gives a wink and takes a swig.

Before I can inquire if legal tender featured in this transaction, the music kicks up again, drowning my concerns in a surge of merrymaking. I sigh.

Through the press of bodies, we head toward the door. The air hangs thick with musk and cheap liquor. Six offers me a drink, but I decline. If I loosen up any more tonight, I'm liable to fall apart.

I hear hooves behind us. A derisive snort.

Figures: Six does the stealing; I do the explaining. I reach to straighten my badge and turn around.

Our mule deer friends have decided to make further jackasses of themselves. "Your friend stole our bottle, batty."

"Did I?" The hare takes another gulp, causing me to wince. "Seems they all look alike."

"Six." I lower my ears to show I'm serious. "Give them their drink back."

A stare flickers between the bunny and I for an instant, then she shrugs and tosses the bottle back to them.

Both deer fumble to catch it with thick fingers and just general thickness. Their antlers rattle together, catching long enough to cause them to spill half of what was left.

Leaving them to untangle themselves, Six and I head out the front door, the dancing stags and the noise of the party fading behind us. We crunch a few steps onto the gravel before I lift an ear at her. "Did you need to steal from them?"

"Wasn't so much a need as a sense of fairness." My thief lectures like a gray-muzzled professor. "They went and hassled it off that kitty, so ah went and gained what they'd ill-gotten."

"It would've been easier for everyone if you hadn't."

"It would've been easier still if ah hadn't gotten caught!"

I groan. We got through, hides unscathed, and that's what matters. I lead her into the twilight, away from the yee-haws and guffaws.

"Hey!" A voice from behind slows us. "Get back here! We'd like a word."

Another voice: "Don't those big ears a' yours do nothin'?"

The deer have followed us. One carries the whiskey bottle, the other nothing but bleary malice.

"Hoof it, pointies." Six spins on a booted heel and jabs a finger their way. "We're not in need a' your sass."

The deer take up positions on either side of us, pawing at the dirt.

My right hind paw itches my left thigh, happening to be near my gun.

They glare. The big one spits, lowering his antlers. "We take exception to that. Do you know who I am?"

She smirks. "Some little pricket who can't hold his liquor."

Having found just the wrong thing to say, Six shoves me out of the way. The smaller deer charges her, rack first, in a clamor of hooves and hollers. My thief hops high, yanking him down by the antlers. The big one rushes forward to assist and gets a boot to the gut for his trouble. Whiskey sloshes from his bottle as it tumbles through the air.

The first one swipes at her with hooved fingers. Six dodges, and hurls him into a post. With a glance around, she smooths her ruffled dress, one paw on a pistol. The deer stay down. Seems she knocked the fight out of them.

With both our drunken foes moaning on the ground, I press a wing to my forehead. "Was that really necessary?"

"Ah was defendin' your honor." She snatches the fallen whiskey bottle from the road and downs the last of it. She tips it my direction with a disreputable wink. "Someday, ah'll have to make an honest lawbat of ya."

"I reckon I'm honest enough."

"Ah figure that'd be the only direction it'd go." She chucks the bottle aside. Ears raised like a cavalry banner, the bunny throws an arm over my shoulders. "Aren't ya glad ah hauled you outta your room?"

I squirm, glancing around. "I think we'd best head back to it now."

"Why? Ya reckon we're plum out of deer to fight?"

I take her paw. "I'd reckon there are things I'd rather do than wander out here all night."

Her ears drop, her grasp closing on mine with an unsteady grin. Once in a blue moon, I do manage to surprise her.

I squeeze her paw a little. "Shall we go?"

Her bravado returns. "Back to that hole in the wall? Bosh! We're going to mah room."

⤋ ⩢ ⤋

Six Shooter no sooner clicks the lock shut than I'm kissing her.

My wings fumble over her body, reacquainting myself with her curves. We lean against the hotel room wall together. It's heaven.

"Mmmmm… Missed you too, lawbat."

I rest my head on her chest. Her scent hides in leather and dust, but I drink it in like exotic nectar.

"Easy there, sugarwings. No need to go nuzzlin' my chest fur off."

I waggle my hips. "You're the one with a paw on my hindquarters."

"Oh hush up!" She swats me on the rump, flustered. "Let me see about gettin' some light in here." She slips from my embrace. A match flares from nowhere, and she lights the oil lantern on the nightstand. The room runs small, but with fine furnishings. Blue enamel washbasin in the corner, plump oak dresser, and a wide, pillowy bed.

The bunny turns, arms crossed over her dress. "You gonna preach at me about stealin' the money for this room?"

I smile. "My lips have other plans."

"Good." The bunny fights a running battle with the voluminous fabric all the way across the room, and only near the bed do I become sure the foe could be overcome. I'd have helped her, but I value my life. Panting in a vest and trousers, finally free from the dress, she seems more a lady than moments before, more my lady. She tosses the garment to the floor.

I pick it up and fold it over a chair.

She seats herself on the bed, kicking her boots up on the fine blankets.

"Six, don't muss up the bed so."

"Ah shelled out twelve damn dollars for this room." Her ears drop, giving me a rush of giddiness greater than any plummet in flight. She smiles. "So why shouldn't I?"

"Because..." I slip in behind her, wrapping her in my wings and delivering a light kiss to her cheek. "...we'll be putting it to good use."

She chuckles, settling in along my body. Kicks off one boot, then the other, letting them flop to the floor.

Her breath and weight feel good against me. One by one, I undo the buttons of her vest. I slip a wing inside, caressing the gentle curve of her breasts. My wing membrane smooths her soft fur and traces over the bare warmth of her nipples. I give both mounds a tender squeeze.

"Mmmmm... Ah tell ya, lawbat, the way you're playin' with those, ya don't seem to mind they're small."

"Mountains might look pretty to some, but hills are where I'd have my picnic." I drape my muzzle over her shoulder, teasing my tongue along her neck to her right breast, toying with her nipple. I take it in my lips and lick with impassioned vigor.

She hums, pleased. Those bunny toes splay against the white bedspread. "Ohhh... That feels nice..."

After giving the same treatment to her left breast, I kiss my way back to her drooped ears, losing myself in the delicate smoothness. My wings slip behind her, exploring the curve of her back beneath the open vest. Smiling like a dreamer, she pulls the garment over her head. Afforded full access, I allow my wings to roam over her slender, powerful body.

By this point, my trousers feel a trifle constraining, but I hesitate to remove them, enjoying this moment. Six seems to be enjoying it too, judging by how her paws drift between her legs, rubbing herself through the fabric. This sight has me pressing up against her, my erection hot and hard against her fluffy tail. I reach down and take over for her, feeling the heat I've stirred up in this bunny. She breathes harder, kissing my cheek appreciatively. After a few more moments, I find myself longing for a more direct approach. Reaching her gunbelt, I rub my wing thumbs over the buckle. She hesitates a moment, glancing to the door. Then with aching caution, she unclasps the belt and slides it from her hips.

My gunbelt joins hers on the nightstand a moment later. I kiss her neck. The vest falls to the floor. Her naked fur brushes my wing membranes. We nuzzle. My wing thumbs trace up her body, down to unbutton her fly.

I slip under the fabric, through fur softer than a daydream. Six moans. I knead the tender flesh of her mons. Her body arcs against mine. My wing thumbs trace around her lips. Pure heat.

My wing thumbs tease their way into her folds. Juices soak them, lubricating my efforts, in and out, deeper and deeper. Her legs spread, her muscles clench and release, her breath warms my muzzle.

"Jordan... Ooh..."

In. "Hmm?" Out.

"W-would ya mind terribly...?" She spares a loaded glance at my lips, and licks her own.

I smile. In. "Taking a shine to that, huh?" Out.

A nod. "That is, if you're agreeable..."

"My pleasure." I ease her forward, onto her elbows. Motion stirs the scent of soap from the blankets. Classy place indeed.

I work her trousers down from her hips. Her tan fur washes out to ivory between her legs. Even in the dim lantern light, it gleams like a lotus. Drawing comparisons to the *Odyssey* my Classics teacher never intended, I set about exploring this blossom with my tongue.

A fluffy tail twitching against my sensitive ears, I lick along both of her outer, then inner lips in turn. Her juices run sweet over my lips as they press in. The bunny on my tongue squirms, gasping my name. Her breathy tone causes a surge in my loins.

I wipe her fluids off my smile, catching my breath. She reaches back, tugging her trousers off. A simple matter of pulling them over her hind paws and she lies nude before me, looking back with vulnerability in her eyes and a blush under her fur.

Freed from layers of cotton, leather, and trail dust, her body's slender and powerful, wound tight as a watch spring. I see about lessening the tension.

My tongue gets back to work for a good while, until I spare glances, musing on her. Watching her body shift atop the sheets in pleasure sends my heart racing. "You're beautiful."

"Don't talk with your lips on me, Jordan." Her ears flush crimson, framing her smile. "Tickles somethin' fierce."

"My apologies, ma'am." I laugh and take the opportunity to remove my own pants. Out of my sheath and erect, my member aches to bridge the gulf between us. "Permit me to make it up to you."

Six's shapely bunny rump sways before me, even as she clutches the pillow before her. "I—uh—can't imagine how a gentleman might go about that."

I kneel closer, my member bobbing up and between her legs. Fur tantalizes my erect flesh. Instinct grips me; I thrust forward, jostling against her clit.

Beneath me, Six gasps aloud and her body goes stiff. The next instant, she's rubbing her hips back against mine. "You'd best see about holsterin' that iron, Sheriff." Her paw reaches up, caressing my shaft, tucking the head inside her.

Pressure and slick heat glide down my member as I enter her. A delicate tension eases through my body, curling hind paws and wing thumbs. I press deeper, the vibration of her moans echo through my chest. Her ears smell of whiskey and her fur of rare nights in her arms. I embrace her, muzzle just reaching her shoulder. Her lips meet the base of my shaft with moisture and the thinnest of fur.

No words pass between us. Six breathes against the pillow, clenching down on me with an occasional shiver. Between my delighted gasps, I kiss the nape of her neck. The bunny ripples all the way down my erection. I whimper, twitching inside her.

Unable to endure this stimulation for long, I prop myself up along her back and give a few needful thrusts. Hot bunny juice seeps around my swollen shaft, dribbling all the way back to my sheath. I whimper again, in a most undignified manner. Before I know it, I'm gripping her waist and am thrusting frantically inside her, bunny style. As one, we murmur and buck, my stiff member plumbing her depths again and again.

"Oh! Oh… Oh Jordan, ya just—mmmm—keep to doin' that."

Never one to deny a bunny, I comply. I ride her to a gallop, wings clutching her midriff. Hare ears swing with every motion. The bed creaks in rhythms sweeter than any fiddle. My sac swings, scattering the fluids running down it.

Tremors of ecstasy trace up my shaft as I bury it once more in my lovely thief. Pulse racing, wings trembling, I whisper her name for it's the only word my mind can formulate, the only concept my heart can hold. I grit my teeth to keep from shouting. Six begins to bang back against me, timing herself to my efforts.

That tail fluffs against my stomach, wiggling each time she hunches against me. Her paws wring the pillow, eyes closing slowly as her breathing quickens. Her pelt catches the lantern light like a statue of living alabaster and sandstone, the narrow slits of color at her half-closed eyes a purer blue than skies have ever known. Never have I seen a creature of such singular beauty and I worship her in the only way fitting.

I'm so close. The urgency of her thrusts says she is too. I run my wings over her bare back, reaching down to perform some gentlemanly service for her clit.

That does it.

She writhes under me, whimpering and thrashing against the bed, clenching on me. Her pleasured gasps haul me over the edge, and suddenly my loins are pulsing, spraying long jets of seed in her grasping tunnel.

"Uuuuuuuuhhhhh! Hah-hah-huuhhh..."

Euphoric jolts shiver through my body, each culminating in another pulse of semen. My ears flatten against my head as the squeak I've bitten back escapes and echoes into the night for all to hear. Around me, her legs try to bounce, but find no purchase, only mussing the fine bedcovers. My wings grip her waist, holding her up and against the surges of my pleasure. I never want to let her go.

All the world's troubles are nothing. In this moment, I'd forsake my job, my duty, my life, all for the hare quivering under me in the aftershocks of climax. In this moment, with all that matters in my wings, I know I could even tell her I love her.

Long minutes pass with us locked in this carnal embrace.

Though exhausted, I summon the strength to lift off her back and pull myself from her. I guide her onto her back, then collapse atop her once more, sticky and sated. The lantern burns low, dancing in her eyes.

Panting beneath me, Six looks up with tender blue eyes, then places a hand along the nape of my neck. I take the hint and lean in, kissing her as hot breath stirs my cheek fur.

I run my wings down her arms, so powerful, so soft. "Is it really so bad being a lady?"

"You bet yer fuzzy tail it is." Her tone rings brazen, but my ears pick up a tremble to it. The bunny under me lays unclothed, but not quite naked. She jostles her hips under mine, speaking softer: "Though bein' a woman… now and then… that ah could come to like."

"I enjoy being the man who gets to see you be one. And live to tell the tale." I nuzzle into a kiss, then pull back, gathering my courage. "The only pity's how rare it is."

I can hear the blush in her voice. "This bunny's gotta know the lay a' the land before she settles it, if you take my meanin'."

"Six, I…" Fear climbs my throat. "I-I don't want to tell you something I'm not sure of yet."

"Hold me then. Say it soft in mah ear as I'm dreamin'." She cuddles closer. "Then I can at least hear it there."

I pull her close. "I want you in my wings, Six. I need you to linger a while if I'm to build my heart around you."

"Not sure as ah can linger how you'd like…"

My heart drops.

"…but ah'll leave as much a' me as I can." She raises her muzzle to my ear. "M-my name is Clarabelle."

My heart soars. I brush my cheek along hers, clutching her tight. She responds in kind, wrapping her arms up over my shoulders. My words can't total up to my gratitude, so I just lie with her, never wanting to let go.

Chapter 10

"Don't be overly so; ya haven't felt under this bustle yet."

I haul Blake to the nectar bee. Truth be told, it wasn't a heavy load, seeing as was less resisting and more just shocked. We get off the train and carry our luggage to the hotel. I'd be opposed to carrying his bags that far, but the lawbat packs almost as light as I do. Seems opposed to the notion of a suitcase he can't fly with, which is a stance I share. Within an hour, we're passing through the bannered gateway marking the entrance to the nectar bee proper.

The crowd mills and squeaks before us, awash with wild color. Fruit bats are nothing if not fanciful. I pause for a moment to look at a paint of a watermelon, only to be informed by the artist that it's painted entirely from watermelon pigments.

The rest of the affair is more sensible, if no less strange. The stalls hold all manner of treats: lemon squares, pecan rounds, and apple turn-overs. Aged wines and fresh lemonades flow freely. Bats of all ages chitter and chirp at each other. I spy the occasional outsider like myself, but a deer here or a hare there is buffeted along on currents of bats.

The bats themselves are dressed in a flurry of colors. The fellas strut about in vests, like Blake, but suspenders seem to be favored means of holding up your trousers. I suspect my lawbat wants to look the part of the heroic sheriff. Meanwhile, the ladies replace the pants with dresses and the suspenders with strips of cloth wide enough to keep them more or less modest. Every scrap of cloth is as bright as the fruit these bats are gnawing on.

At the far end of the festivities, a cluster of stalls sell canned fruit by the wagonload. More than one fruit bat family is squabbling about just what sorts will serve them best. Jars of cherries, peaches, and plums glimmer in a glass rainbow as they're loaded to and from carts.

Blake excuses himself to go have a peek at the wares. I stand by a juice booth's shaded lattice, which the customers dangle from, sipping drinks through those newfangled wax-paper straws. We're hardly at the shindig half an hour before Clementine swoops in on us.

"That's the sheriff? You modest thing. Fragile's hardly a word I would apply to him."

I narrow my eyes at her. "Yer puttin' me on."

"I most certainly am not." A flap swats my arm. "Any more sinew on that frame and he wouldn't get off the ground."

My glance casts about the crowd, catching on a fruit bat in being harried by a butterfly, shooing it away with scrawny wing fingers as he retreats with a coo of dismay. A gaggle of gangly bat youths pass, stuffing their muzzles with ripe bananas and chattering. "Reckon that's true." I nod. "Hadn't stacked him up against many other bats."

"Quite a stack, if I may say." She takes another sip of wine. "The ladies of the bee may never forgive you."

I mull that over a moment. My eyes track down the lawbat, who is chatting graciously with a cluster of bats, mostly young ladies. They're busy fawning over his every word, admiring his badge like it's the only star in the sky. My lower lip takes on a jealous slant.

A rather plump fruit bat bumps past me, smacking on a strawberry kebab with open enjoyment. He's looking a little like a berry himself, puffed up inside that ruby waistcoat. His ears only come up to my chest.

My nose gives a sullen wiggle. "And to think ah troubled Blake over the little peaches done in needlepoint on his vests."

"The world assumes we can't embroider." A quick wiggle of her wing thumbs, then she shakes her slim muzzle. "The trick is to get a good, comfortable chair so you can keep your feet free for it."

That notion frees a laugh from my chest. "Ah have a sudden urge to get mah lawbat some yarn and knitting needles."

Clementine sidles up beside me, a glass of red wine held delicately between her wing fingers. "How are you finding the nectar bee?"

"Reckon it's about the fruitiest function I've attended." I nod up at a flutter of flying fox kits bouncing through the crowd, each dressed more like a gumdrop than the last. A couple of weary parents flew after them, clad in vivid paisley. I squint. "Colors are a mite stunning."

"Covers up the fruit stains." The wine in her cup swirls, glinting in sunshine. "Your suitor seems to be enjoying himself."

I blush to the ears at her comment. Nobody's ever called him my suitor. "He's awful easy in a crowd. Guess he breathes a little easier when he isn't busy being the only force of law in a day's ride."

We watch as one of the fruit sellers wedges a peeled prickly pear into his muzzle. Sticky pink juice runs in rivulets down his dainty chin as he compliments the vendor.

My ears lift in amusement. "A creature a' high society, that lawbat."

Some little fruit bat stands off to the side, staring me down as he chomps at a cantaloupe. Could stand to slow down, judging by the swell of his cheeks. I lock eyes with the kit, who can't be a day older than five and wearing an outfit with too many ribbons and buttons to ever have been chosen by a kid. Just as I'm starting to feel some sympathy for the kid, he finishes the melon slice and sticks his tongue out at me. Then he flutters off, dripping. His wings, or maybe even the melon rind, whack my left ear, leaving a sticky mess.

Hopping mad, I shake my fist after him. "Yew'd better fly, ya little fruit brat!" I grumble, wiping it up with my sleeve. "High society mah eye..."

Now it's Clementine's turn to laugh. "I will admit: it lacks the refinement of the opera, but nectar bees have a charm all their own." She stretches her wings, which catch a soft glow in the afternoon light. "And they don't require a lady to wear anything overly starched or layered, which I am fond of."

"I didn't find the opera excessive in its expectations of finery." I stop my blabbing about how. I was dressed as a man at the time, after all. "Granted, now, we were up in a box."

"And the good sheriff seems the modern sort." Her wineglass lifts toward him and me in turn. "Courting a hare—and one who speaks her mind, no less."

My chuckle comes out a touch nervous. "Yeah, the lawbat's a patient one, alright." Haven't had much cause to consider it before, but Blake does treat me about the same in trousers or in a bustle. Makes me somewhat more inclined to wear a dress. Still about as inclined as desert flats, however.

"Our grandparents might have had a fit about such things, but this is the nineteenth century." Her tone brightens with ambition. "How's he feel about women's suffrage, if I may ask?"

"Hm?" In spite of the occasional sticky bat fluttering overhead, my ears rise again. "He's opposed to mah sufferin' generally. Ah endeavor not to make the boy suffer too much either."

"The vote, Ms. Haus." She looks at me askance. "Would he begrudge you participating in democracy?"

Oh, right: we can't do that. I add that time I voted for Blake to stay sheriff to the list of crimes I've committed. "Can't say it's ever come up."

"Really? I'd have thought it would be a topic of conversation for a couple like you." Her wings cross as she gets a trifle cross herself. "I'd assume a woman like you would be out protesting at every election."

"I elect to have a drink." I buy one from the same stand she did.

My suffragette companion straightens up and turns a little toward me, though her voice still drops a little whenever someone walks by. "If we don't take a stand against the patriarchy, how can we expect men to listen to us?"

I ponder if dynamiting Hayes' mine counts. Decide against mentioning that. "True. Never have seen the sense listenin' to them, though. Known more than a few to get carried away by their emotions." I take a sip. It's smooth, if painfully sweet. "Come to think of it, not sure ah trust menfolk with the vote."

She tosses her head back in a squawk of amusement. "I shall mention your stance on the matter the next time someone tells me I want too much. Makes my position seem like quite the compromise."

I shrug. "We are the fairer sex."

Lo and behold, Blake returns to us. His wings tote two bulging canvas bags. Setting them down with a clatter, he smiles at me.

"Ya got some kinda juice on yer cheek." I touch my own to show him where I mean.

"I'm lucky that's all the damage I sustained." He dabs at his muzzle with a white handkerchief of surrender. "I scarcely escaped with my wallet."

"Ya got fruit back in White Rock." I bump an elbow at him. "Ah've seen yer pantry."

"They have blueberries!" His foot snatches a jar of purple preserves from one bag. "I've been having raisins with my breakfast for months."

My eyes roll. "Just how ya survive on the frontier, ah'll never know."

He twirls a wing to the other flying fox. "You going to introduce me to your lovely bat companion?"

"Sheriff Jordan Blake, this is Clementine Zephyr."

"Lovely to meet you." He bows and kisses her wing fingers.

She giggles as she curtsies. "Charmed."

Lawbat rises with a look of pleasant surprise. "I didn't know you had friends in town."

I raise my eyebrows at him, but decide not to take offense. "Ah didn't. Just happened to bump into each other downtown and got to talkin'. She put me on the trail of this nectar bee business."

"Well, then I have you to thank for this excursion." He flashes a winning smile. "Now if the town hasn't fallen to pieces when I get back, this will have been a successful vacation."

Again, I move to rest my palms on the handles of my guns. "Yer first, if memory serves."

"Success being qualified, of course, as no one shooting at me."

She titters. "Goodness, Mr. Blake. It's a wonder a lovely lady such as Clarabelle has the mettle to let you go out on your own."

"Her metal is half the problem." He smirks at me. "Iron, most often."

Clementine laughs. "Well, I'm afraid I must leave you two to each other's mercies." She snapped open a slim wooden case and handed me a calling card. "I hope you'll stop to visit next time you're in the city."

The card gleams like a little square of civilization in my dusty paw. "It'd be mah pleasure. Ah'll even try to drag the lawbat along with me again."

She gives a polite little bow, then sweeps her wings wide and launches off with a graceful flutter.

With a glance at at the setting sun, I give a heavy sigh. "Suppose we should be gettin' along too, if we're gonna make it to the hotel by dark."

"Too true, I'm afraid." Blake bends to sort out his purchases. "Well, imagine: you spent several hours engaged in polite society. And, I daresay, not much of it was horrible. Umm!" He strains to lift the bulging sacks of fruit.

I grab one and sling it over my shoulder. It clatters as I straighten. "Not much."

Blake wraps the remaining bag in both wings and manages to follow, only looking a trifle unbalanced. "I'm impressed you didn't feel the need to carry firearms."

"Don't be overly so; ya haven't felt under this bustle yet." I give my tail a little shake his way.

His ears drop at the scandal. "One step at a time, I suppose."

"Ah'm liable to gun down a chair at this rate. Don't expect to see me in this getup all the time. A bun's gotta return to her ways sooner or later." I cast a look at him sidelong. "Was nice to see ya in yer natural habitat."

His ears rise. "What'd you mean by that?"

"In a high-class crowd, yammering on about poetry, art, music, juice…" A smirk touches my muzzle. "Don't see why ya left it all behind to play sheriff in a dustpan like White Rock."

"Sometimes dreams pull one in opposing directions." He sidles up next to me. "Though I do appreciate a certain bunny's company."

His tone sets a burn to my ears like a shot of strong drink. I watch him from the corner of my eye. "Ah'm not much for talkin'."

He laughs. "On the contrary, I've found you always have something to say."

"About how to fit a saddle, sure. Or maybe what whiskey pairs well with a saloon brawl. But philosophizing falls outside mah territory."

He cocks an ear. "I shall endeavor to bring up some philosophical quandaries for you."

"Ya bring up enough." I laugh. "Like 'how could he possibly need this many little fancy vests?' But now ah know."

A moment passes in quiet as we saunter past the thinning crowd. "I do appreciate this, Six."

"What? The fruit?" I cast him a coy look. "Imagine mah surprise."

His muzzle shakes, with a smile. "No, that you're endeavoring to learn more about my culture."

"Just keen to make sense a' ya." Both ears drop to my shoulders. When he watches them like I hoped, I smile.

A grin brightens his dark muzzle in return. "I have a little surprise too." He shifts the bag to one wing, placing the other around my waist. Guess there are some other benefits to wearing dresses, aside from the refreshing draft to my nethers.

"Dare ah ask?"

The lawbat puffs up a bit. "The territorial governor is on tour, including a whistle-stop in White Rock. I have it on good authority he intends to thank us for retrieving that gold."

My ears rise at the notion. "With cash?"

"With words." He rolls those gold-flecked eyes. "And probably some manner of recognition ceremony."

I narrow my gaze at him. "So in return for takin' yew to this ace-high party, you're gonna take me to a boring one?"

"Boring perhaps, but I think you may find the fashion sensibilities more to your usual standards." He pats my lower back, clattering the revolvers hidden under my bustle.

We walk together, arm in arm.

Chapter 11

"You just soaked the territorial governor like a fruitcake."

Evening light gilds the town. Weasels wind down the street like dust devils, two of them orbiting a third, who is waddling under the weight of a generous jar of pickled eggs. They chitter under a badger teetering on a ladder, who is attempting to string a "Welcome to White Rock" banner across the street. The squat decorator snaps at them, causing the trio to traipse all the faster. The fennec telegraph operator peers out from his office, apparently not getting news fast enough down the wire.

The lawbat paces around his office. "Governor Terrence has a reputation as a fickle creature." He fidgets his wings. "I need this trip to go smoothly."

Leaning back against the wall, I kick one boot to its toe. Most buns hop around bare-pawed, but I cotton to the poses boots lend me. Bats, of course, never see the point in shoes. "Something in particular ah should do?"

"Just keep anything untoward from happening." His little wing fingers check his star's on straight. "I could deputize you again, I suppose."

"Ah'll pass." I cross my arms with a smirk as he ambles by. "The nights are pleasant enough, but ya always insist on leavin' the office at some point in the day."

His pretty ears fly straight up. Turning away, he straightens his smart red vest, embroidered with green leaves and yellow mangos. He glances at his reflection in the window, back to me. "I would take it as a kindness if you didn't fluster me before the governor arrives."

I lean in and nibble at the backs of his ears. "Lawbat, this is only the start of mah flusterin'…"

He squeaks and flitters away. "On second thought, just abstain from scoundrelism for one evening." He pulls on his moon-white hat, brushed clean the night before. Before I flustered him, which was the only way to get him to stop carrying on about this visit. Pity we don't have time for that presently.

"Don't want me showin' up the political on scoundrelism?"

"Not when he's here to thank us." With a deft flick of one hind paw, he checks his pocket watch. "I'd better get to the station. Wouldn't do to be late."

"Ah'll go to ground." I place my paw over my heart, then give him a little kiss. "Don't worry yerself so, Jordan. If anybody's square enough to please this straightedge, it's you."

A little smile sprouts on his foxy muzzle. "I shall take that as the compliment you meant it." With that, he pads out the door. "I'll come get you for our congratulatory photograph." A sweep of his wing drags the door closed with just the pull of air.

For a long moment after, I stand in his quiet office. Watch out the window as he vanishes up the street. Let him deal with that stuffy old governor—I'm quite content with my own company. The clock on his wall ticks on, marking time. I check my mismatched pistols twice, clean some dirt from a claw, then surrender to the notion of going outside. Plenty of places a hare can wile away the hours without raising a fuss.

↓ ↯ ↓

I know full well the lawbat hates when I make trouble in his town. Doubly so with this government bigwig around. I keep my paws clear of the glad-handing and guffawing by Blake and the doc foxes as they give him the town tour. Likewise avoid every drop of drink at the saloon. Take great pains not to cheat at the poker game.

Turning out being lucky makes folk think I'm cheating.

Just my luck.

"Good-for-nothin' card-sharpin' bunny!" The lynx yowls at me, slashing with chipped and dirty claws. "Quit yer bouncin' around!"

Having no intention of heeding the kitty, I hop over the bar and swing by a rafter out the saloon doors. Don't stop outside either—I bound up onto some fancy varnished carriage rolling past. From there, it's an easy jump to the roof of the bar. Hot wind and hotter sun greet me. Panting through a grin, I chance a look down.

My feline pal prowls out, dagger-tipped ears pricked. Now I just have to wait on him to leave. I let my breaths unwind, heartbeat slowing.

Sheriff Blake flutters on over, lands at the steps of the saloon, and looks straight up at me.

Unlucky lynx follows his gaze. Right to me.

Curious how I'm so fond of a lawbat whose main joy in life is making mine not go smooth.

Lynxie snarls his way back into the saloon, demanding the proprietor get him somehow up here to join me. That old collie barkeep ought be able to deal with him, I hope.

A small crowd collects from the passersby, like pebbles falling in a creek.

Blake waves a wing at me. "Six, get down here—you're causing a scene."

I sigh. The boy never understands how much he complicates matters. Not even a bunny's keen to jump off second stories, so I aim for a two-wheeled cart delivering spirits.

I land with a thump, spot-on, only to discover the cart not affixed to any pony. This small matter causes the cart to pitch forward; a number of casks to take flight. A barrage of whiskey barrels pummel the street and onto that duded-up carriage beside it. The cart's owner, who had been securing his wares, wrings his naked tail in horror.

The lawbat watches like I just squashed his favorite sort of fruit.

"Sorry about that, squeaks. This oughta settle matters." I press my poker winnings into the paws of a sputtering liquor salesrat, ambling over to the fruit bat with a swagger in my stride. "Buck up, sheriff." I pat him on the wing. "Nobody got clobbered."

From the wagon emerges a terrier, wringing the whiskey from his ace-high suit.

I hear the lynx scampering from the bar, so I spin and give him my mean look.

Kitty takes off running, bob tail bouncing as he skedaddles.

Pride swells in my chest. Not every bunny can stare down the rougher sort of feline. With a chuckle, I turn to see Blake wearing his serious face.

The chill of excitement clings to my chest, though my ears do their best to soak up sun. "What're you all sour over, Sheriff?" I touch his wing with as much tenderness as is wise in public. "Ah paid for the damages and everything."

Looking for the source of the drink, the gussied-up terrier sees to cussing up a tornado's worth of profanity.

Blake presses a wing to his face. "You just soaked the territorial governor like a fruitcake."

With a sigh, I present my wrists for shackling, having the feeling that I'll be spending another night in the town jail.

⻊ ⺇ ⻊

Got to watch Blake explain how he'd arrested me—I did my best to make him sound all brave-like in his story—then he excused himself to take me somewhere I might be less of a threat to the territory's terriers. Soon find myself in the familiar confines of the jail cell attached to Blake's office. Out of the sun, I start to cool off, though I can't say the same for Blake. He's giving me a big talk about how it looks bad when a drizzle of the who-hit-johnny hits elected officials, like I'm not aware.

I sigh, leaning on the bars. "Lawbat, don't ya reckon you're makin' a pity out of a peach pit?"

"You expect me to believe you're innocent in all this?" Leaning against the bars from the other side, he refuses to look my way, leaving my very good attempt at batting my eyes for naught.

"Even ah've gotta be innocent once in a while." I excuse myself from his handcuffs, slipping them back onto his belt. Blake's never been good at making the law stick in matters of me.

He glowers at the far wall. "He thinks my town is in chaos. If I hadn't pawned him off on the foxes, White Rock would be looking for a new sheriff about now."

"Oh Blake, it all worked out." I chuckle, then rest my chin on his shoulder through the bars. "No harm, no fowl, as the birdhounds say."

He ignores me, but doesn't shrug me off either. "I know several birdhounds who'd dispute that."

"Hush with your lawyerin' a moment. Ah'm trying to think up a way to set things right for ya." My claws trace the etchings on my father's gun at my hip, my other paw fiddling with the blued replacement at my other. I reckon Blake disarms other criminals he throws in here. "Ah could go committin' some crimes and pin them on folk we know are criminals anyhow—"

The lawbat tugs his hat low against the baking sun streaming in through his office window. "No, Six."

I tip a finger his way. "A bun could steal enough gold to make an plaque in the shape of the territory and—"

His muzzle touches mine, just a little. It's soft, like his softening tone. "Are you fully incapable of abiding by the law?"

"Not fully…" I shrug, my paws wrapping his waist. "Ah'm abidin' by a number of laws this very moment."

He sighs, slacking against the bars. "I can't let you out while the governor's still in town."

"Reckon that's reasonable." I kiss him under the jaw. "But how's a bun supposed to make this up to you?"

He moans, unaware I'm borrowing his keys. Handcuffs are one thing, but the heavy iron lock on the cell door would make a corkscrew of the lockpick I keep in my boot. Lawbat turns, and for a moment I think he's caught me red-pawed, but then he just cups my face in his wings. "Don't stir up more trouble. Please? Governor Terrence will roll out of here at sunup." Those pretty brown eyes sparkle in afternoon sunshine. "We'll talk later."

I smile an innocent bunny smile as his lips press to mine. For a moment, I consider hanging the key ring from my tail, but tuck the keys into my gun belt instead. Idle wings are less likely to find it there.

Blake breezes out of the office, launches off the porch rail, and flutters into the evening sky.

Swinging the keys around my finger, I ponder sitting in the cell until he returns. Could stay here and not make the situation any worse. But I reckon I could make it better faster out there. Never have been one for waiting around.

I unlock the cell.

Well aware the bat could spy me from above, I slink out his bedroom window and down an alley. I find the governor in a change of clothes and in conversation with the foxes. The good sheriff flutters in with a string of apologies, then swoops down beside them. From a distance, I watch as they yammer and yap for a while, but Blake's duties catch up to him: the local collie barkeep and the liquor rat come to him with some manner of dispute. They drag him off, leaving just the medical foxes to finish the tour.

With the fruit bat once more out of sight, I meander on past the babbling vulpines and set my plan into motion.

ⱶ ⚳ ⱶ

An hour later, out the saloon window, I see the lawbat swoop down next to Deputy Harding. He lands, sweeping out a circle of dust in the lantern light. The bloodhound sniffs his way up to the front door and points me out. That foxy face pops up through the merrymakers, ears up. He casts a gaze over the crowd to get an idea of what's going on.

The terrier's too short to see, but his glance sticks on my ears like a cocklebur—and is about as prickly.

I raise a shotglass at him. His key ring dangles from my paw. "Here's to our dear lawbat! The only sheriff who coulda reformed me in a few scant hours."

A general cheer arises.

Grumbling, he weaves his way inside, no doubt intending to give me an earful of undiluted opinion. As he arrives at the bar, though, his wing is clasped by eager paws.

The governor stands before me, all four and half feet of him. "Sheriff Blake! I must say, I had some real reservations about the job you were doing. But your dear friend Mister Shooter has explained this whole misunderstanding."

"S—" He forces a cough. "He did?"

"Oh yes." The little grey dog nods, wire-hair whiskers angled by a grin. "A finer gentleman I couldn't hope to meet."

"Now there's a subject for debate…" He levels a gaze on me.

"Tracked me down just to buy me a drink and apologize. I had no idea he was seeing to a leak in this very roof." He points a grey paw up.

The collie barkeep stops examining a shiny gold coin and slides another drink the governor's way, avoiding my eyes.

The terrier takes it, wincing as he attempts to down it.

My ears swivel. One paw drops to my sliver gun. An instant later, I remember to set my other paw on the blue steel one as well.

Tension grips him. Lawbat's eyes follow mine.

A lynx leaps in from the side. His black claws streak toward me. "I'll show you, bunny!"

Blake lashes out with a hind paw, grips the feline's ankle, and yanks. With legs in two very different directions, the cat collides with a table, then the floor. The resulting wallop hits the lynx in the diaphragm. He coughs a blast of cheap whiskey over the floorboards, then crumples. Still holding on, he twists the cat's leg out of kick range.

The lynx yowls a string of profanity colorful as a peacock's plumage and twice as lurid.

The governor yips through the last of his drink. His dainty hind paws skitter on the wood floor beside the collapsed cat, his ears erect. "Good heavens!"

"See, governor? Ah was tellin' you about how this lynx is always causin' trouble. Can't get a moment's peace in this town." I smile over my glass. "Thank goodness for Sheriff Blake."

The terrier nods, appeased, and lifts his glass. "I'll drink to that!"

The lawbat buries his face in a wing, only to have it dragged down by the governor. He flashes everyone a pained smile, still holding the struggling feline by the ankle. With a sigh, he draws his handcuffs and snaps them in place with his wing fingers. He allows me one round of libation in honor of my own cleverness before conscripting me to help carry the profane feline to my now-vacant jail cell.

☇ ⩕ ☇

I help the lawbat throw our feline friend into the lockup. My fruit bat remains sour, of course, even as I talk him into the bedroom. Once there, he dangles from a rafter like an unripe kiwifruit.

Certain time will sweeten him, I sit on the bed, just to be at eye-level, legs crossed.

He crosses his wings, candlelight flickering on chocolate pelt. "You're pleased with yourself."

I lean on my knees, flashing him a coy look. "Who'd 'a thought a little more whiskey was all the governor needed?"

His look stays a trifle bitter. Those powerful hind paws clamped on the rafter.

My ears drop. I sigh and stand, knowing it's time to shoot straight. "I'm sorry, Jordan. You know trouble follows me like a cocklebur. Figured the least I could do was get it out of your fur."

"You caused all the trouble in the first place." He flickers amusement my way, dangling at my waist. "This makes us even?"

"No..." I pad over, laying a paw on his crotch. Our eyes meet and he gives me more tingles than a mountain of mirror ore. "...but this might."

He looks up at me. Lawbat always has the best surprised looks.

While his brain's still catching up, my fingers dance through the buttons of his fly. I part the fabric, letting his bits flop down, then nuzzle down his shaft. My paw closes around his base, guiding him into my lips.

Blake gasps as I breath on him some.

Bending down a little, I take him in my mouth. My lips close over the warm head of his erection. My eager tongue traces into his sheath, playing along that shapely head. He's so warm, and getting warmed up, swelling bigger with every heartbeat. I suckle him deeper, stroking his delicate wings.

The sheriff moans, nuzzling my thigh, a little creak coming from above as he digs into the rafter. The head pulses, hot on my tongue. "Oh Six..."

"Mmmmm..." His taste, all sweet and musky, tempts me deeper onto him. I find myself drooling more than's ladylike as his shaft slides past my lips. My ears burn with bashful lust, swinging back and forth against his stomach.

Lost in his flavor, I scarely notice as he undoes my belt. Wing thumbs hook my pants, dragging them down. His slim muzzle noses into my undergarments, long lovely tongue tracing my folds like the most tender fruit.

I squeak around his shaft, then hurry my pants off my ankles. With a wider stance, I spread wide enough for him to slip inside. I shudder, feeling him swirl inside me, before I remember where my muzzle is.

He licks deeper, bottom lip rubbing my clit. Pleasure catches like wildfire, raising a haze of pleasure across my mind. Fruit bats have unfair advantages in these matters. I'm getting wetter than a mad hen down there, and he's just getting started.

Not keen to be outdone, I collect my dangling ears. I rub the shaft, feeling the give of his skin as my ears slide over it. His warmth clings to my night-chilled ears. His balls bounce off one side of my ears, our wetness collecting on the other.

The lawbat's groan shivers into my loins. His tongue twirls like a twister, sweeping joy into my every little fold. His lips wiggle against my slit, setting a tingle to my clit and a shiver to my spine.

Gripping his cock for support, I gasp around the head. Each heartbeat chases the last, every breath catching the next. My muscles clench on his slick efforts. I shudder.

My muscles flutter along his tongue as I call out his name. Might have come out a trifle clearer without his penis in my mouth, but I reckon he got the message. Hare juice floods my passage, dripping down his muzzle, which my hips seem trying to bury. All patient and smug, Blake dangles, swinging with the force of my climax, that tongue still wiggling all four sides of a square dance inside me whenever his nose bumps my slit. Quivering from the inside out, I clutch him close with desperate elbows, unwilling to let go of his shaft, too fond of how it feels wrapped in my ears.

When at last my pleasure starts to fade, he draws free of my tender bunny burrow. I collapse onto the bed, slipping off him with a slurp so loud and so lewd that I'm sure the lynx in the clink must have heard it, if not the whole town. My ears sweep back, trying to hide their blush.

The lawbat grins and wipes his mouth, reaching to the rafter with one wing before swinging down on it. That firm length bobs all the while. Can't blame a bun for staring, what with it being so pretty and bouncy. It glistens in the flickering light, wet all down the sheath as he comes close. As if that weren't worth the price of admission, his hind paws do the trick of pulling off his trousers. He stands before me, so fond and still firm.

I take him in my paws, feeling the blush creep up my cheeks as he

dribbles a little from the tip. Stroking his sheath over the throbbing flesh, I look up into those coffee-brown eyes, the eyes that keep me awake nights. Drunk on the feelings still squishing through my slippery folds, I kiss the top, rubbing him, craving his release.

Those tender wings rest on my shoulders, hips jerking forward and bumping inside my open muzzle. My tongue wiggles of its own accord and, though I'm no fruit bat, I must have done something right.

The sheriff shudders, wing digits gripping tight. His length pulses hot, rich salty-sweet juice into my waiting mouth. I smile at the taste, lapping it up with greed that'd fluster a prospector. Another shot, then another, then a small series of dribbles. I suck, trying to encourage them, but a whimper from the lawbat stops me. Letting him slip free, I give him a few spare licks and a look up.

He cups my cheek in his wing, like he's real fond of me. I smile like a dope, then come to realize some of his juice just dripped from my smile onto him. He doesn't mind, though, just kisses me like we're right proper and falls into bed with me.

As warm wings draw me toward sleep, just like I've been dreaming of all these weeks, I reckon being lucky's not so bad.

↓ ↯ ↓

Lawbat'll take any occasion to dress up. He's got raspberry-red trousers under a orange vest I've never seen before; it shimmers with some manner of leaf pattern, gleaming in the sunshine.

We're standing at the side of the little stage. The governor yips and yaps his way through a speech about how we're the Frontier's engine of progress. I half-listen, wondering just how he thinks this bunny-shaped cog fits in.

Half the town's turned out, shading themselves with parasols and fluffing their fur with fans. Must be a couple dozen of them in a clump before the stage, with more standing under shop awnings to either side of the street. White Rock seems to be making a day of it, to the point that even a swindler or two has shown up to relieve them of their hard-earned dinero. I watch the snake-oil hawker with particular interest, as he might need a taste of his own medicine.

Charlotte and Doc Richards stand to either side, fur copper and postures mayoral. The governor calls us up from his podium, taller than I remember. The foxes leave to make room for us. As I bound up the steps to the platform, I can see a wooden crate's been provided to elevate him above the common folk. My boots clatter along the dry boards, carrying me to a spot a little behind and to one side of the canine in a tailored coat.

Blake flutters up onto the stage, then sidles next to me. He puffs up with importance. Slight thing that he is, I'm not entirely assumed he won't blow away on a sudden gust.

I bump an elbow on his golden vest. "Crêpes, lawbat, ya look like marmalade."

He fakes a little laughter out the corner of his muzzle. "You could have dressed up." He nods toward the governor. "This is a formal event."

I step a little closer to Blake. "Ah reckon someone has to balance out your finery."

Governor Terrence makes waggish jokes to the crowd, who clap and chuckle. Not exactly a barnburner, but it fits the bill. Beyond the terrier, I watch as the raccoon cameraman makes some final adjustments to the accordion bellows of his device.

A gleam flickers out of the pocket of his fancy little vest. He passes it from his feet to his wings, then waves it before me. "I polished your pin."

I tip my hat to him. "Much obliged."

He fixes it to the breast of my overcoat. Having someone touch my bosom in public is something I avoid, generally, but I figure I can trust the lawbat at this point. He finishes and dusts my shoulders. "Someone has to keep you looking respectable."

I shrug and give him a grin. "You're welcome to try."

He tips his muzzle up at the camera, eyes forward even as he grabs my paw. This is concealed behind the governor's back, but still makes me blush. "Smile, Six."

With a wave to the governor, the photographer ducks under a black cape to peer up at us.

I swallow my shock and force a grin. The camera clicks. I let my bunny instincts take over and freeze me in the Arizona heat. A couples seconds later, he pops back out from under the cloth and gives us a chatter of approval as he preps the glass plate for development.

The fruit bat releases my paw and walks up to pat the governor on the shoulder. The foxes pop back up to start chatting with the both of them. The crowd slowly scatters. I let myself get carried away in it. Plenty of time to pounce the good sheriff once the hobnobbing's done. I may be a scofflaw, after all, but I have the scruples not to sink to the level of politics.

Chapter 12

There she lays, smiling, naked as a jaybird and armed to the teeth.

On the wing in the desert wind, I squint against the glaring sun. Frilly panties flutter in my pocket.

In the distance, the governor's stagecoach leads a dusty trail out of my town and back toward Phoenix. Not a moment too soon: Six had vanished just after our commemorative photograph with him, followed shortly thereafter by a visiting charlatan's valuables. No sooner had I assured the reputable businessmink that I'd investigate it, than I was scrambling to hide from him a blatant display of lady's undergarments left on my desk.

I flutter to land above the ruined mine, sun clinging to the membranes of my wings. Heat shimmers off the bare-stone mountainside. Picking my way through the rocks, I slip into the shadow of an outcropping and turn to take in the view. Far below, my town lays out like toy models, complete with a gaudy-painted wagon rumbling out into the desert.

From the shade behind me, a voice—smokey and amused: "'Bout time you got here."

I draw the bloomers from my pocket and, stepping into the cool of the shade, hand them over in the least scandalous manner possible. "This is your idea of an invitation?"

"Reckon they got the point across." The desert hare takes the garment from my hind paw, setting them aside as she lays back down. "Ah am a mite disappointed ya didn't show up in 'em."

"Is that what a pair of bloomers on my desk means?" My wings cross. "I'm afraid my education only included the secret language of fruits and flowers."

"Point was they weren't on me." Her paws flick down her vest, unbuttoning.

I crossed my wings, waiting as my eyes adjusted to the dark. "And you stole from that snake oil dealer, didn't you?"

"Aww, sheriff, you know ah'd never sully mah hands robbin' some common swindler." She kicks one boot off, then the other.

I sweep a wing at her. "You're laying next to his strongbox!"

"That?" She glances at the pried-open lid. "That's a product a' pure, honest thieving—not robbery."

"He said someone made off with his wares too." A quick look around reveals no such items, though she could have them stashed elsewhere.

The bunny slips her socks down in two graceful motions, revealing shapely lapine legs to me. "Besides, he brews his stock from tobacco juice and bottom-shelf whiskey. Even ah wouldn't drink the stuff."

"You can't just loot the wagon of every passing mountebank."

"Just for you, Blake, ah'll fix to loot other things." One deft paw undoes her belt, whipping it off with a sharp crack and a sharper grin.

"I have have half a mind to arrest—" My mind skids to a rough landing. "Are you…disrobing?"

"Ah'll stop if yer set on arresting me." Hare fingers dance down her fly before she shimmies those slim hips free of her trousers. Her fur shines in the evening sun, naked from the gunbelt down.

I stammer, coming as undone as her outfit.

She giggles, drawing her hat off those long, delicate ears. "Aww, law-bat. Way you stare, you'd think my clothes'd never excused themselves from our presence before." Propped between two rocks beside her, a wine bottle sits half-empty.

I close my eyes a moment, trying to remain focused. "So you not only stole his money, you took his half bottle of wine."

"It started out a full bottle, but you took half the day gettin' here so I thought I'd try it." The bunny, near to naked and basking in the heat, nods in the direction of the evidence. "You ever open one of those with a bowie knife? Had to drink half the thing to get rid of the cork."

"You are the height of chivalry."

"Like a knight in armor." With deft coordination, she removes her vest, exposing the subtle curve of her breasts. There she lays, smiling, naked as a jaybird and armed to the teeth. "No lawbat a' mine's chokin' on cork chunks."

I sit beside her with a sigh.

She touches my leg, studying my face.

Putting my wing on her paw, I give her a smile meant to reassure.

Her confidence falters, her free arm covering her chest as she glances anywhere but at me. "You'll have to forgive a bun for being thin on practice, but I was seducin' you just now."

"I noticed." I grip her paws with care, lifting her into my wings. For a time, we sit like that in the shade of the outcropping, my wings around her nude form.

Hare fur tickles my wing membranes as she ducks her head a little. "I can put my clothes back on. Was just tryin' to get a rise out of you."

"Oh you did." I shift my hips, trying to ignore the tightness of my pants. "Believe me."

She chuckles into my shoulder. "Hotter 'an blazes anyhow. We can wait until sundown." Desert air sets a sway to the dry grass that clings to the side of this cave. Her gaze flicks down toward sunlight and what passes for civilization. "Unless you got official sheriffin' to do."

I squeeze her tighter. "I'm where I need to be."

Her voice breezes soft and hot, like the desert air. "So we can compromise on you holdin' me?"

I nod. She turns to lay against my chest, still under my wings. We sit, hiding from the heat, breathing each other's scent. The sun dips lower, stretching out the shadows and creeping into our refuge.

"Six...you know I think you're grand." I settle my chin in the crook of her shoulder. "I've even been willing to overlook some occasional larceny. But, as far as I've seen, you don't need the money. What's your plan? What do you want out of life?"

Her ears rise with mischief. "A burrow under the whole a' the West. Filled with gold." She nuzzles the inside of my elbow in a most distracting manner.

"The truth, Six."

She blinks, turning to look me straight on. Lightning crackles in those stormy blue eyes. "What'd you want me to say? That I want to settle down on a little farm with you and wear frilly dresses?"

"I see no reason that we can't live to a ripe old age wearing trousers together."

She looks about to say something, then swallows it. Her ears drop, draping over my wings.

"This isn't about dresses. Or thieving. And I don't want you bare-pawed in the kitchen. This is about you dying alone in the desert because you finally annoyed somebody you couldn't outrun." Cold dread grips my heart. "And me never finding out."

Silent, she tugs my wings closer around her. Moments pass as the sun kisses the horizon. "Ah don't set out to worry you... Thought ah said as much."

A groan of frustration leaves my muzzle. "I acknowledge we've covered this ground before." I give her a chance to consider, then soften my voice. "Are you coming to town over and over waiting for something I'm not doing?"

"No!" She turns to me again, ears pinned back with surprise.

"Then what is it?"

"Ah don't rightly know." The bunny squirms, trying to escape the topic.

"I'm not saying I don't want you—I'm saying I want you enough to be a bit selfish."

Her paw brushes my cheek, looking in my eyes. "Is what we've got really so bad?"

"Yes." I take a deep breath, my chest and my stiffness pressing against her. "Just tell me the truth."

A sigh and she closes her eyes. I see the little muscles of her ears and face work as she ponders instead of just talking. At last, her naked body slumps against mine, gunbelt jabbing me. "Ah... Ah'll think on it, Jordan. You got mah word."

"Thank you." I kiss her cheek.

Her eyes glint the amber light, her forehead touching mine. "Yer lucky you're pretty." I get the distinct impression she's forgiven me.

I am a fool after all—my beautiful lady friend throws herself at me, naked, and I ruin the moment by talking. Granted, if she'd gotten my pants off any faster, we wouldn't have this problem.

I let my wings trail along her stomach. Her fur sweeps warm under them, even as the air cools, somehow soft and coarse at the same time. My eyes wander from the pink of her nethers to the pink of her nose. "Could I say you were beautiful without getting shot at?"

She smirks, but I can see her ears redden. "Ah guess that'd depend on where your lips were when you said it, lawbat."

I press my lips to her collarbone. "You're beautiful."

She gasps.

Her neck. "You're beautiful."

She groans.

Her ear. "You're beautiful…"

Our lips meet. The wine's lingering spirit leaves her tasting like exotic fruit.

My wing digits stroke through her fur, my palms cupping the delicate curves of her bosom. I play with the tender flesh of her nipples. The kiss deepens as I curl my tongue around hers.

She giggles backward. Sunset swims across her face. Her fingers tease under my vest, then unclip my suspenders. They and my vest soon join her clothes on the floor of the small cave. Her touch paints my wings with soft-furred affection.

A blush creeps under my fur, as I let this lovely hare reacquaint herself with my body. She vanishes for so long that it takes a little while before her return feels real. I spread my wings, every inch of me welcoming her touch. The sun's final rays set my wings aglow, casting us in ambers richer than even the evening.

Those skilled paws unbutton my fly, then dive inside to my straining shaft, furred fingers caressing my sensitive tip. They dance swift as shadows up and down my shaft. Kneeling further, she tugs me out into the fading light. The cooling air contrasts with the warm reception I'm getting. She kisses the soft folds of flesh where my sheath has pulled back. Those big blue bunny eyes glance up at me. "Feelin' good?"

I cradle her cheek ruff. "Mmmhmm."

Her ample ears pin back with happiness. With a titter of delight, she plants a kiss right on the tip of my glans.

My body shivers, a faint pulse of fluid traveling my length to her lips.

The bunny eases back, the faintest gossamer string of precum connecting her smile to my erection. She lays back on her bedroll, hooking her toes atop my pants and slipping them down. Legs spreading, her hands trace along her gunbelt. "Wanna help me outta this?"

Stroking her muscled thighs, I uncinch the buckle, slipping free the dusty leather. With an arch of her back, I draw the gunbelt aside with care, turning my attention to the unclad bunny before me. My kisses start at her lips, that velvet nose twitching in anticipation. Then on to her nipples, stiffening pink delights in her creamy fur. Then down her soft stomach to her softer folds, her legs tensing as my tongue delves into the deepest kiss yet.

A halo of twilight flares through her fur as she writhes in pleasure. Her heels scribble slow patterns of delight into the gravel. Her slit burns with damp desire against my mouth. Those slim hips rise from the bedroll, fluffed tail brushing my chin.

I hum into her. My tongue swirls within her, collecting the taste of her delicate nectar. Eager wings stroke her stomach. An even more eager appendage throbs beneath me, bobbing in time with my licks.

Somehow, I'm still wearing my hat, which she squashes over my ears with a squeak of passion. Her muscles wring my every lap. A hot clitoris bumps me in the nose.

Moving up, I suckle that tender nub.

A gasp of surprise. She shivers, toes wiggling against my wings. Her grip tightens, pressing me into the jerking bucks of her hips.

My tongue dances along her walls, my lips worship her swollen labia, prolonging her muted climax. Her fluids soak my muzzle, leaving it sticky. My tongue starts to tire; polite bat society would lament at how out of practice I am.

Six seems not to mind, panting and limp, her heartbeat pulsing against my mouth.

I sit up, doffing my dented hat and extricating myself from the trousers riding up under my sac. Crawling atop her, I grip her shoulders, tracing one wing thumb across her cheek.

A paw on my back draws me into a tender kiss. She opens those bedroom eyes, giving me a look of dreamy longing.

Not one to refuse such a lovely lady, I reach down, dragging my member through the luxurious fur of her midriff and into the slick, yielding flesh of her slit. My hips ease forward, entering her with a single, unsteady stroke. Pressing into her, I feel a heat purer than the desert, with a moisture it could never know. I always forget how wonderful she feels until these very moments. Her silken walls part, slick with passion and slackened with pleasure. Her passage welcomes me with teasing clenches, hips trembling upward as I press a moan from her body.

We work up a rhythm, gravel crunching under her bedroll. She strokes the fur at the nape of my neck, urging me to thrust faster. That poofy bunny tail bounces up at my sac. She bucks up at me, whispering for more.

I ride her hard, trying to bury every thought of tomorrow in the slick immediacy of her passage. We clutch together on the bedroll. I thrust atop her, inside her. The bunny squirms on my girth, whimpering in joy. We move as one, basking in the wonder of each other's flesh.

One paw grips the scruff of my neck, the other rubbing her nub against my plunging shaft. The bunny yelps in ecstasy, muffled by my shoulder. Her passage clutches, fluttering along my length.

I redouble my efforts, my sac slapping against the wet fur of her crotch. As she comes down from her climax, I feel her gripping my shoulders. Her smile lights the twilight, shining pure desire my way. The familiar rush of pleasure, too long denied, surges inside me. With my last thought before orgasm, I slam hard into her. My balls jump, throbbing thick bat seed up my shaft. Spurt upon spurt jets into her, spraying her quivering walls. The slick feel of my cream rushes over the head of my penis, painting the hare's tunnel with fresh passion.

Six wiggles, simpering in giddiness as I pump her full of fruit bat essence. Her long legs hook over my back, her body rocking, squishing our juices between my still-spurting member and her squeezing walls. Her own orgasm tapers off, but the hare seems quite pleased about me reaching my peak.

As the final trembles of my orgasm shudder into her, I collapse. Her body wrapped around me, her scent everywhere, I bury my face in the fur of her throat. My breaths come easy and deep. Aftershocks leave us twitching against each other for some time.

We lay there, soaked in satisfaction and steeped in each other, until night finishes stealing the day's heat and starts on our own. Keeping me in her arms, she rolls sideways and tugs the bedroll around us. I slip out in the process, spreading our juices along her thighs. The tall bunny holds me close, her body atop mine.

My lips meet hers in a warm kiss as we secure the bedroll around ourselves. Starlight shines in her eyes, setting my soul ablaze. Whatever else comes along, I know I care about her and that she cares about me. I stroke her back in the cold night. I could ask her to stay, but she won't. She could ask me to follow, but I can't. So instead, we lay soaked in the heat of each other's bodies, holding each other close enough to forget being lonesome.

Chapter 13

"You mean to say spirits in that metal ball drove the thieves toward my town?"

Sheriff Jordan Blake, City Office, White Rock, Arizona Territory
Four bandits evaded capture today. Wounded my best men. Two-pony
wagon headed your way. Well armed. Red bandoleers.
Sheriff Thaddeus Callahan, City Hall, Scoria Grove, Arizona Territory

The telegram flutters in my wing fingers as the fennec telegraph agent trudges back through the wind. I close the door, sealing the dust currents outside, then pad back to my room.

In the scant moments I spent seeing to the knock at my door, Six has rolled and lit a cigarette, which she smokes in my bed, naked and lovely. The curls of smoke trace upward, white and subtle as the curves of her body.

I wave the slip of paper. "From the sheriff in Scoria Grove."

"Inquirin' on your taste in dresses this season?" She tosses me a coy glance, beautiful and infuriating.

"Some roughs got past him. Could be trouble, Six." I try not to lose myself in the subtle slopes of her body. "They're headed our way."

"Bosh. Ah'm trouble." Snatching up her gunbelt, she grins my way around a smoldering cigarette. "And ah'm headed theirs."

I sigh. This woman might well be the death of me, but, watching her dress beside my bed, I can't bring myself to complain.

Ꝓ ∾ Ꝓ

With the ponies saddled and Six as decent as she gets, we look to the horizon. Dust devils kick up, then wither to nothing in the hot afternoon sun. Together, we mount up. My pony is only now getting used to my hopping aboard with a flap of my wings.

Harding hands me a shotgun. "First round is birdshot. Gets more serious from there."

"Thank you, deputy." With care, I slip it into its scabbard on the saddle, slung low horizontal enough my feet can reach it from riding or standing. "Once we warn the outlying farms, we'll loop back to town."

The bloodhound shrugged the rifle slung over his shoulder. "I'll be on the saloon roof. Ought to smell anybody coming. Wish we had a clue as to species."

I hand him the telegram. "As do I."

Six stirs her bay pony. "We gonna sit around jawin' all day?"

I tip my hat to the deputy and click my tongue. My mount trots onward, toward the edge of town.

The hare canters up beside me with a glance down at the longarm. "Reckon I should get a scattergun? One of those little hogleg numbers? What'd they call 'em?" She snaps her fingers, a noise as soft as the fur on her paws. "Lámpara? Se para? Se embarra?"

"If you're referring to some manner of obscene lamp, perhaps. If we are talking about the gun made famous by Italian wolves, the word is 'lupara'." I roll my eyes and Rs. "And you require neither."

She smiles. "Just thinkin' of yer safety, lawbat."

"So am I."

"Just stick closer, sugarwings." Her ears droop over the brim of her hat. "That'll keep you outta the line of fire, among other benefits."

I stiffen in my saddle and snap my gaze forward, trying not to let her see me blush. It's going to be a long night.

� ⚡ �

Evening light hangs long shadows from every rock on the landscape. We alert several homesteads, working our way up Skull Creek, toward the mountains. Old Camp Mountain, the nearest, can be identified by the massive crack blasted in it. Six grins at it.

With miles and hours wearing on, I dig out a strip of fruit leather to nibble on. I'm halfway into the wax paper, when I notice rare silence from my hare companion. I glance over.

Ears up, the bunny watches something come around the bend of a hill as we plod on. One paw on a silver revolver, the other on a blue steel one, she scowls from behind her kerchief.

Not many things in life manage to quiet Six, so I look the same direction.

A two-pony wagon stands abandoned. Before it, a feline body lies in the dust. Rust-hued dust clings to the wet hole on its coat. Around its chest wraps a red leather bandoleer.

I dismount, finding the cat is cold dead. My eyes meet Six's. "In-fighting?"

One paw traces her revolver. "Would reckon so." Those ears rise further, aglow in the sunset.

My wing thumbs tighten on the reins. "What?"

Six stiffens, spreading the sides of her duster like wings. "We are a mite surrounded."

I pause, then hear it too—at least three men, positioned around us. I click a few times, to confirm their locations, then clear my throat of dust. "Gentlemen! The name's Sheriff Jordan Blake." I flash my badge to the scrub-covered hillsides. "I have reason to believe you men are in possession of stolen property—"

Shots crack, whistling past my ears.

Our ponies scream.

Beside me, Six bounces up from her stirrups, then off of her saddle. An instant later, I watch in awe as the bunny spins high above me. Pistols flip to her paws, then flash half a dozen shots.

Not eager to get shot again, I drop to the earth.

The ponies panic and thunder off. I roll out of their way. The shotgun bounces from its scabbard and tumbles to the ground, a couple yards off.

Her boots land beside me, only to skitter sideways as bullets bite the dirt around us. She spins to snap off three more shots with her silver gun, the steel one forgotten, then freezes, ears attentive, a wisp of smoke curling from the weapon.

Silence looms as everyone hangs fire. All around, I hear moaning from the brush. Three forms writhe in the bushes.

The bunny holsters the empty revolver and helps me up. "Ya ask after ya shoot 'em."

Brushing the grit from my fur, I try to shake the ringing from my ears. "New gun working out?"

"Like dancin' with one foot asleep." She turns the weapon over in her paws, contemplative. "But ah muddle on somehow." After clearing her throat, she addresses the shrubs. "Gentlemen! Ah have reason to believe yer now in possession of a number of my bullets. If ya feel this isn't adequate compensation for yer abidance, do speak up."

A wordless roar rips over the desert.

A grizzly's massive frame rises from the hillside. Tattered clothing hangs off his frame. Claws shine bloody in the dying sunlight. He hunches, then roars forward. Hind paws churn soil, ripping gouts of sand free. For all his bulk, he tears through the dust toward us.

Six's ears drop. "Aw blazes." Pistol flashing level, she backpedals, shooting. Her first shot craters in hard earth, while the next two wing the brute.

The towering ursine doesn't even slow, rage lit in his eyes. Those claws slice gleaming arcs, each an inch from her retreating form.

I draw and unload my revolver into his legs. Half a dozen shots, three hit.

The bear staggers, then spins on me with a roar, a quarter ton of undiluted fury.

A brown overcoat falls over his head.

The bunny bounds up his back and bashes both gun handles on his skull. The crack of metal on bone rolls like thunder over the desert. A roar of pain and fury follows.

Scrambling back, I bump into cold steel. The shotgun.

Massive claws rend the coat to tatters. The towering ursine rounds on her. With a wild swing, he backhands her guns, knocking them away. Swipes of those gleaming claws catch her shadow as she bounces back. Snarls and profanity lash out, but she stays a bounce ahead.

I snatch the shotgun with my wing, toss it to my feet, work the lever action, and level it on the bear. A slow exhale as I wait for my thief to spring clear, then I unleash a volley into the bear. The birdshot bounces off his hide, so I pump the lever and fire again, this time followed by the sickening patter of buckshot into flesh.

Hit in the shoulder, the ursine staggers to one side, but roars after the hare.

Taking advantage of my slowing the great brute, Six snatches the bowie knife from her belt, grips it in both paws, and braces her boots in the dirt—wide open to a killing blow.

A crushing swipe arches down on her, only to be impaled on the foot-long blade. Buried to the cross guard through his palm, it erupts from the back of his hand like a monolith of steel and blood. The bear bellows at his wound in confusion and horror.

Six swings a savage kick to his temple, which hits like the thump of a ripe mellon.

The brute drops. Dust rolls out from the impact.

Still on my back, I snap another round into the shotgun and train it on his writhing form. "Six?"

The hare snags her silver pistol from the dust, reloads with cold ease, and draws a bead on the groaning heap of fur. Past her boots, the shreds of her jacket tremble on the indifferent breeze. Her bare arms catch the last glints of sunlight as she flexes a sore paw. "I liked that coat."

⊻ ⩘ ⊻

A solid click proclaims the security of the cell door. Inside, the bandits sprawl on the floor, bandaged and drugged. The sharp cloy of ether hangs thick in the air. Here and there, one of their number offers a hazy groan.

"I managed to piece them back together." Doc Richards washes his paws in a basin, then casts a serious glance to Six. "You did a real number on that bear."

"He's lucky it wasn't a bigger number." Boots kicked up on my desk, the bunny cleans her bowie knife with a smug gleam. Her wrist is wrapped: a minor sprain. "Fella seemed a mite keen on dividing me."

"That bear has to be seven feet tall." With an eye in the jail, Charlotte packs the remaining medical paraphernalia. "Is the cell going to hold him?"

Harding nods, ears bobbing. "Those bars run into the foundation and close over the top."

Strolling from my desk, the hare bends to adjust her boots and just happens to kneel beside the possessions we removed from the bandits. Those deft paws poke through the belongings.

I strive to ignore her. Often, she steals things only to bedevil me. "I don't like putting them all in one cell, but it's only until the marshals arrive."

The vixen fluffs her bottlebrush tail. "They won't be in a state to cause much trouble, even when the ether wears off."

"Call us over before you give them anything, even if it's just laudanum." Doc waves a black paw at the prisoners. "I've been reading some papers on drug combination—"

"Glad sakes!" Six laughs a victory cry. "Now that raises an ear or two..." Her muzzle buries further in a small brown diary, blue eyes wide.

A sigh drags itself from my bosom. "Six, dare I ask what you are doing?"

Fingertips held to her chest, she fawns up at me. "Oh, beg pardon, Sheriff Jordan Blake." Still kneeling, she mocks a bow. "Ah reckoned at least one of us could be useful and find somethin'."

I close my eyes. "Just read what you found."

"Ahem: 'April 6th. Hayes didn't show. Tempers on edge. Could sell the thing, but don't want to cross the lion. Best just to keep it.'" She beams up at me. "Glad sakes, seems ah have a nose for investigatin' after all." She wiggles it my way.

"Anything else?"

She flicks through few newer entries, then reaches blank leaves. "Nothing about Hayes." She moves to pocket it.

"Pity." I pluck the book from her paws. "That's evidence."

"Hey now!" She rises to make half-hearted attempts to retrieve it from me. "Ah filched that fair and square."

I thumb through the entries, sparing her only a miffed glance. "You haven't a square bone in your body."

Charlotte shrugs to her husband. "Well, that's medically true."

Six taps a finger on my badge. "How in blue blazes am ah supposed to hunt down that lion if ya interfere?"

"You said yourself it contains no other mention of him." I slip the journal into my waistcoat, where she is unlikely to reach with the foxes present. "Perhaps once our guests convalesce, they can enlighten us further."

She scowls. "That ruffled lout could be back in the Old States by now. Or imposing his sweet self on the jungles of Africa, for all we know."

My wings cross. "And the law can't lay a paw on him unless we're in possession of evidence."

"Ah'm possessed of a powerful need to wring Hayes like a dish towel..." Her ears droop to a sulk, at least until she chances upon the outlaws' gunbelts.

I turn to the vulpines. "Still no news on Hayes, Doc?"

"Afraid not." The todd scratched his white, whiskered muzzle. "Though I can't say that's a bad thing, strictly."

A quiet moment passes. I resign myself to having a jail full of unhappy criminals for the next few days. My office is already rather small, but I wonder if it could stand a partition between the bars and my desk. Alas, that would mean being unable to see the occupants, so I abandon the notion.

Six, meanwhile, finishes restocking her gunbelt from the pile of confiscated bandoleers, then ambles out the door. The foxes don't bat an ear, too focused on their patients.

I've known her long enough to not trust her slipping out unannounced. Excusing myself, I follow.

Outside, under the light of a lantern, she's poking through the bandit's wagon with a ne'er-do-well grin.

I reassure the ponies tied up outside with a brush of my wing, then sigh at her. "Six, kindly refrain from further pilfering."

She turns, her subtle curves no longer hidden under a duster. "Now Blake, nothin' under the sun didn't once belong to somebody else."

"It's evidence." Seeing no point in trying to stop her, I walk up to at least witness the tampering. "It belongs to you even less than most things."

"What have we here?" She hefts a shining metal box, as big as a phonograph player. Fanciful etchings tumbled around its perimeter. "Ya know what's so fine folk'd stick it in a gold box?"

I tuck my thumbs into my belt. "I haven't the faintest."

"Neither do ah." She flashes me mischief's own smile. "Let's find out."

Six lifts the lid, freezes a moment, and collapses like a sack of potatoes.

My wings sweep around her, breaking her fall. The box bounces off the back of the wagon, spilling open, and ejecting a metal sphere the size of a small melon. Moonlight and lamplight dance over its etched surface as it plummets. In a split second, I snatch it with my foot before it can hit the ground. It's heavier than I thought —as is Six— but I manage to hop my way back into the City Office with some measure of dignity.

Dragging in yet another unconscious gunfighter stirs an understandable vulpine hubbub.

The medical foxes dive to dote over Six. Charlotte checks for a pulse, then looks in her eyes. "What on Earth—?"

"Mirror ore." I heft the orb onto my desk with a thump.

Doctor and deputy turn to it with shock and shocked recognition.

Doc Richards stands to appraise it. "I've never seen a piece that size."

"I have. In coyote villages." Harding strokes his jowls. "They use them to speak to the dead."

I get my first real look at the sphere. It's been hammered or carved with incredible precision, layer upon layer of detail drawing the eye around and in, forever in. I blink. My gaze flicks to my thief, limp on the floor. Unable to abide seeing her helpless, I duck outside, grab the gold box, and place on my desk. With care, I seat the orb inside.

Richards stands to study the orb with a scholar's dispassion. One dark paw strokes his chin, then opens toward me. "You think our bandits were affected by this ore nodule?"

Under my wings, the box closes with a velvet whisper.

Six jolts up from Charlotte's arms and hollers: "If you 'yotes'd hang yer yammerin' for one blue-blazin' second—!" She glances around, accusation and embarrassment in her stormy sapphire eyes.

The foxes and I do her the kindness of ignoring her.

Ears flat, the vixen glances at her husband, then over the unconscious criminals. "More than likely, I'd say."

ᘯ ᗯ ᘯ

Harding rides ahead, kicking up dust with his scruffy nag. Overhead, the sun burns. The only sign of civilization is the occasional cairn

on a rise. At least, I think they're cairns. Could be natural rock heaps. Our bloodhound guide seems to know where he's going, though.

Under the shade of her hat, Six glances to me. "Reckon White Rock'll survive without us?"

I shrug. "We did deputize Doc before we left."

She rolls those fiery blue eyes. "Best we return 'fore that goes to his head."

"I... I'm glad you're alright." Swallowing back a break in my voice, I ride on. "I worry when you get reckless like you did with that bear."

"Worry I might not, lawbat." With a flourish, she draws in a blur of silver, spinning a revolver on one finger and not even slowing to shove it back in the holster.

I straighten the reins in my wing fingers. "You ought to practice with that new gun."

Her tone dulls. "Ah ought to get my other one back."

Not for the first time, I admire her subtle curves from the corner of my eye. "You always seem to wear the silver one on your right side."

"Do ah?" She looks between her guns. "Hadn't drawn mah notice."

I lift an ear. "Are you left-handed?"

"Might be." With earnest curiosity, she spins the shiny revolver from one paw to the other. After a few whirls to and fro, she shrugs. "Tough to say. Reckon ah knew, once." She holsters.

I look for that thin, familiar smile on her, but find her muzzle plain with sober consideration. I wonder sometimes what goes on in her head. Never put much stock in echoes —falling into that hazy limbo between theory and wishful thinking— but the evidence does pile up. My thief would not have survived her own recklessness this long without some kind of unseen aid. Desert air buffets my wings as we scale the mesa path, tempting me to lift off from the saddle and fly.

On the pony she stole from me last year, Six smiles my way. Sunlight glows through her ears as if through the finest sheet of marble. "Don't go blowin' away now, lawbat."

I haul my hat down over my brow, fighting the wind. "I'd manage quite well on the wing, thank you."

Ahead, Deputy Harding turns his sad bloodhound eyes to me. "'Yotes aren't so used to flyin' folk. Might not be keen on you dropping into the middle of their affairs."

As we crest the slope, a sandstone cliff rises into view. At its base, a lush plot of squash, corn, and beans grows along a series of irrigation ditches, fed by a small but steady stream. A few small buildings poke up from the fields.

I look up.

An entire town scales the cliffside, carved from the rock and sculpted from adobe. Multiple stories loom over us, windows open to the wind, interiors dark. We stop in a packed dirt courtyard.

The deputy casts a howl to the dry wind.

First one howl, then a few more in unison comes as the reply, an erie chorus in the dry wind. I see no one, though tending those crops would take at least a few dozen pairs of paws. At the center of the plaza, a figure rises from the earth. Dust dances around her form, sun gleaming from a worked silver necklace. Her stride flows like a rolling river across the dry landscape. Glass and turquoise beads clatter in her hair. "Welcome, Harding." Her voice carries a hint of the howl from moments before. "To what do we owe this pleasure?"

Harding's tail thumps the saddle. "Come into possession of your property. Came by to return it."

A tinge of amusement colors her yellow eyes. "Join me in the kiva." Light cotton dress rippling in the breeze as she turns back to the opening in the dirt. A woven and dyed satchel bounces at her hip.

Dismounting, we follow her down a wooden ladder to enter some kind of tiny pit-house. Shade and cool air greet us. The space forms a rectangle half the size of my office. The floor, composed of the same adobe as the cliff dwellings, has a round hole for no purpose I can discern. I look back the way we came, at that minuscule square of sky.

Six snickers at me. "They're as keen on down as you are on up."

I let that comment breeze by. Best not to encourage the bunny in front of our esteemed host.

The 'yote leader sits on a mat, directing us to do the same. "Make yourselves comfortable."

After seating himself cross-legged, Harding opens the sack, pulls out the gold box, and places it before her with no small reverence.

Her slim, tawny paws trace along the lip of the box, opening it just a little. The 'yote sways. Harding stills. Six's eyes glaze over. I slip a wing behind her, ready to catch her again.

The tan canine closes it once again. "The bandits raided a village nine days ago. My people worried these killers, these thieves, would destroy the Ancestor Stone." She sits up, cool as the shady enclosure we're sitting in. "It is good you have returned it. That worry could have lead to rash action."

"We visited a little rash action on them ourselves." The hare tries to find a comfortable way to sit on the folded blanket. "Why didn't you see to them yourselves?"

"We are farmers, not warriors." The coyote sweeps a gesture up toward the crops. "The desert does not permit such excess. We do have certain other assets, however." Her paw reaches into the bag.

I lift a wing and fan the notion off. "I returned this as an officer of the law, not for a reward."

The 'yote gives a coy chuckle and presses a paw to her chest. "We wouldn't insult your honor with earthly wealth."

The bunny raises a point with her index finger. "Y'all can insult me with earthly wealth."

From her satchel, she draws a beaded cloth, then unrolls it to reveal heavy parchment. "Our treaty with the settlers forbids violence against them."

Six's ears rise, as does the corner of her mouth. "So ya just let folk run off with your plunder?"

"We did." A slim smile appears on her canine lips. "The ancestors did not."

"You mean to say spirits in that metal ball drove the thieves toward my town?" The question comes out more incredulously than I hoped.

The coyote nods. "Yes."

I cross my wings, but don't dismiss the notion outright. "Well, I wish I could say that's the strangest suggestion I've heard recently." Clearing my throat to get our host's attention, I lift a wing toward the box. "I wonder if you might tell me more about the mirror ore."

The 'yote ponders a moment, distilling her thoughts. "To the uneducated, it appears to be simple silver. It is more. The spirits of the dead pass back into the Earth, which is why something from the Earth is tied to them. That is why we value it."

The bunny nods. "Couldn't help but notice the fine box ya got for it."

"Echoes cannot reach us through gold." Her paw pads trace over the gilded case. "That is why we value it as well."

Six reins in a laugh. "Thought ya liked hearin' from the clearly departed?"

Her paws fold atop her lap. "Yes, but the living must also live."

The bunny elbows me. "Good thing ah've been collecting a little gold here and there."

I roll my eyes. "Good thing…"

"All that wisdom ought to give ya an upper paw more often." Six shines a little grin in the shady room. "Not hidin' in holes."

Harding and I both groan.

The leader's yellow eyes gaze down a long muzzle. "The ground is to us what the sky is to you, hare: a portal to the eternal." Those pointy 'yote ears dip back. "And our ancestors' wisdom worked very well until you people showed up with all your new problems." Her tone levels out. "But the ways of my people do not change with the fashion like yours do. Forgetting our ancestors, and their stories, would deprive us of their aid. We must be keepers of their memories. Listeners for their wise whispers."

Six shifts, long legs crossed. "Ah've been known to do a little listenin'."

"But only a little." I mutter, unable to stop myself.

The 'yote regards her in silence.

The gunslinger's paw rubs down her long ears. "Can't say it helped overly, beyond gettin' a word from my pa here or there."

My own ears rise. It's rare the bunny sounds serious about anything. Even rarer to hear her talk about her father.

The canine straightened her silver necklace. I notice for the first time that a tiny copper tortoise gleams among its charms. "But he lends you his skill." Her yellow eyes examine the bunny's expression deeply. "Doesn't he, Listener?"

My thief freezes, tense with surprise. Her fingers trace that silver gun, but along the hammer, showing no inclination to draw.

A woof of amusement echoes in the cool dark. "I thought as much. Try not to join your father too soon, and you might gain more than just quick paws."

Thoughtful silence settles over the hare. Her brow furrows over a steely gaze, as if she can't decide whether to be angry.

I fidget. My wing fingers slip into my pocket, feeling something smooth. I draw out a coil of glass seed beads, the most lurid hues we could find at the general store. "Oh, I almost forgot." I offer the beads to her. "I thought bringing a gift would be neighborly."

Breaking from her contemplation, Six scoffs at my attempt at diplomacy.

I keep my tone cordial, my continence serene. "Some guests bring things instead of taking them."

The coyote accepts the offering and appraises it with a merchant's eyes. "Thank you. I feel we should be neighborly too."

ψ ∾ ψ

An hour later, our ponies plod along, crunching along the desert soil. Hot breeze whips dust in our faces and makes the ponies skittish.

The bunny pouts. "All that work for nothin'."

"It wasn't a total wash." I glance back at the bunches of colorful peppers peeking from our saddlebags.

"Don't know if ah trust these 'yote peppers." She peers at the fruit. "They're all scrawny and wrinkled."

"They've grown them for thousands of years." Reaching back, I pop one into my mouth, puncture it with my teeth, and let the slow burn seep out. A fruity undercurrent adds body to the fiery sear that spreads over my tongue. "Oooooh. And it shows." I munch down a couple more, savoring the tingling heat.

Six plucks an angry red one and glowers at it. The tiny, wrinkled red fruit gleams like fresh blood in the sun.

I wave a wing to caution her. "Weren't you paying attention at the opera? Bat cuisine can be spicy. You should probably start with a little piece of the green ones."

"Ah shoot whiskey, smoke tobacco, and reckon ah can handle any little pepper you're chomping like raisins." Her smile gleams like stolen pearls.

The deputy slows up, turning to watch. His tail thumps the saddle again.

I lift a wing finger. "Six, I wouldn't…"

Her paw waggles the pepper in front of her muzzle. Defiant, she chomps into it. Her ears drop in an instant. She spits out the bite, followed by a string of profanity black enough to darken a crow.

Harding and I can't fight back our laughter. For all the heat and all the danger, life out here has its moments.

🡇 ⩊ 🡇

A month later, she finishes a spot of target practice out by the creek. I've never known her to practice before, and even now she only bothers to practice with the replacement gun. A half-dozen cans perch on various rocks, only to get plinked down one by one as she empties the Colt. Each shot cracks like thunder, rolling in an echo between the boulders.

She's been here over a month. She's starting to look at the road like she used to look at me after a month gone. Her ears go up at my approach, but she just looks down to reload from the rounds in the loops of her gunbelt. The casings vary in color, no doubt some raided from my supply.

I lean against a nearby boulder. "Sure been nice having you around for more than a day here or there."

The bunny freezes for an instant. "Sure has." She snaps another few bullets into the cylinder.

Moments pass, bittersweet. I clear my throat, muzzle aimed out at the horizon, even as my eyes remain upon my thief. "You in the wind again?"

She frowns and holsters. "You fixin' to talk me into stayin'?"

I sigh under the weight of truth. "Couldn't if I tried."

Those blue eyes shimmer to mine. "And if ya could?"

I shake my head and slip tender wings around her. "I want to hold you, not hold you back."

She nods between my ears. "Offer still stands to tag along."

"When you need me to watch your back, I can vanish for a day or so without the town falling to pieces." I brush a wing along her arm. "Any idea when you're coming back?"

She leans down, her forehead pressed to mine. "When ah'm tired of looking over my shoulder."

"And what maps will you be unrolling?"

"Find some ancient ruins that don't get mah dander up." She shrugs. "Maybe have coffee with Clementine."

I turn to her. "You're going looking for Hayes again."

She hangs her head as she draws back a bit. "Wouldn't forgive mah-self if he melted the gun down to spite me. Especially if ah were getting comfortable instead of getting a move on."

I nod. "What happens when you get it back?"

"Couldn't say. Hop that gap when ah come to it." She takes out a square of paper and taps loose tobacco onto it. "Imagine you'll be involved."

"If not implicated." My wing fingers linger on her elbow.

"Ah'm comin' back." Deft paws roll the paper. "Ah'm not done with you, Jordan."

An updraft of hope surprises me, lifting my muzzle level with hers. "Nor I with you, Clarabelle."

With the strike of a match, she lights up and gives me a cigarette smile.

Epilogue

"She's wearing our friend James' old pin."

Rain patters over the lush foliage of my family estate.

I sit in the covered patio, unbothered. The gardens need it, and it paints such lovely pictures with the morning light. I smooth my dress and have a look at the newspaper, one of a selection I subscribe to from the West. It's out of date, but that can't be helped: it had quite a distance to travel.

That's when I see the photograph.

Rising, I sweep into the manor house and across the dining room. My hard-heeled shoes clack along the wooden floors. The old canine butler steps to one side, allowing me past.

Taking a breath to gather myself, I straighten my whiskers and jacket. The heavy double doors swing open under my palms. My ears brush the doorframe as I advance.

After an hour on the porch, the sitting room feels uncomfortably warm. A fire crackles like popped knuckles in the hearth. Paintings of my various, deceased, relations stare down from the walls, unimpressed.

In the chair facing the rain-streaked window sits my mother. She's motionless, but I don't think for a moment that she's daydreaming.

I round the chair and approach, paper in paw. "Mother?"

"Eudora." She leans forward and grips the pommel of her cane. Sapphire eyes cast me a sharp glance. "To what do I owe the pleasure of you brandishing broadsheets at me?"

"You should see this." I reveal the page in question to her. The photograph shows a little grey terrier in a tailored suit shaking the wing of a bat over recovered gold bars. Beside them, and taller by far, stands a hare with genuine pride and a counterfeit smile.

The elder hare twitches her nose with consternation. "You're certain?"

"I recognize my own child." I point to the shoulder of the old coat the bunny is wearing. "She's wearing our friend James' old pin."

"Dear daughter, you could spangle me in teetotaler trinkets, but that wouldn't make me a temperancette." Her head inclines toward the liquor cabinet, which shone with all the colors and polished angles of a jewelry box.

"And Jasper's pistols." I skimmed through the article. "Mining explosions, gunfights, and some nonsense about giant scorpions."

"Oh my." Her gaze darkened out the window. "That does sound like Jasper's progeny."

"Seems she's fooled the town with her masculine persona."

"She has been allowed to play tomboy long enough." Her ears rose, one faster than the other. "People are starting to talk. We can't say she's away at finishing school forever, especially since she's liable to be half-feral from wandering the desert."

"I intend to pay her a visit."

"See that you do. Make her as presentable as you can on the train ride home." She flexed her paws atop the varnished cane. "I would retrieve her myself, were it not for the rheumatism."

I cleared my throat and called to the dining room. "Jiles?"

At least three pairs of feet shifted outside the door. A polite delay later, the butler poked his head in. "Yes, Ms. Eudora?"

"Pack my things."

He nodded. "How long will you be gone, madam?"

I take one last look at the paper in my hands. "As long as it takes to get to Arizona Territory."

Other books by Tempo

Sixes Wild: Manifest Destiny
First book in the Sixes Wild series.
Cóyotl Award winner for Best Mature Novel of 2012. Spur Award nominee for Best Short Novel of 2012.

Windfall
A tale of mystery, suspense and otters.
Cóyotl Award and Ursa Major Award nominee for Best Novel of 2015.

Allison & The Cool New Spaceship Body
An interactive sci-fi novel about transhumanism, AI, and growing up.
Coming soon!

More words by Tempo

furaffinity.net/user/tempo321
twitter.com/tempo321
sofurry.com/tempo